THE WOMEN'S WAR

JAMES PATTERSON is one of the best-known and biggest-selling writers of all time. His books have sold in excess of 325 million copies worldwide. He is the author of some of the most popular series of the past two decades – the Alex Cross, Women's Murder Club, Detective Michael Bennett and Private novels – and he has written many other number one bestsellers including romance novels and stand-alone thrillers.

James is passionate about encouraging children to read. Inspired by his own son who was a reluctant reader, he also writes a range of books for young readers including the Middle School, I Funny, Treasure Hunters, House of Robots, Confessions and Maximum Ride series. James has donated millions in grants to independent bookshops and he has been the most borrowed author in UK libraries for the past ten years in a row. He lives in Florida with his wife and son.

BOOK**SHOTS**

STORIES AT THE SPEED OF LIFE

What you are holding in your hands right now is no ordinary book, it's a BookShot.

BookShots are page-turning stories by James Patterson and other writers that can be read in one sitting.

Each and every one is fast-paced, 100% story-driven; a shot of pure entertainment guaranteed to satisfy.

Available as new, compact paperbacks, ebooks and audio, everywhere books are sold.

**BookShots – the ultimate form of storytelling.
From the ultimate storyteller.**

THE WOMEN'S WAR

JAMES PATTERSON

WITH *SHAN SERAFIN*

BOOK**SHOTS**

1 3 5 7 9 10 8 6 4 2

BookShots
20 Vauxhall Bridge Road
London SW1V 2SA

BookShots is part of the Penguin Random House group of companies
whose addresses can be found at global.penguinrandomhouse.com

First published by BookShots in 2016
This edition first published in BookShots in 2017

www.penguin.co.uk

A CIP catalogue record for this book is available from the British Library

ISBN 9781786530844

Typeset in 9.88/13.5 pt BerkeleyStd by Jouve (UK), Milton Keynes
Printed and bound in Great Britain by Clays Ltd, St Ives Plc

MIX
Paper from
responsible sources
FSC
www.fsc.org   FSC® C018179

Penguin Random House is committed to a
sustainable future for our business, our readers
and our planet. This book is made from Forest
Stewardship Council® certified paper.

THE
WOMEN'S
WAR

CHAPTER 1

Two years ago

WHILE ALL THE OTHER girls in kindergarten would doodle pictures of ponies and rainbows, I would draw myself parachuting out of helicopters and landing on dictators. My little stick figure would karate-kick twelve other stick figures, somehow making them explode in the process, and then I'd aim my portable missile at the obvious target: a dragon.

Nearly thirty years later, I'd be a Marine Corps colonel riding on a Huey. The only difference between the girl in my crayon drawings and the real me is that I didn't have a parachute, I'd use rope. And the dragon caught in my crosshairs wasn't a big lizard with wings—he was a little lizard with total dominance over the US–Mexican narcotics trade.

His name was Diego Correra.

We were midflight, northwest of Diego's location, which was a compound tucked in the outskirts of a Mexican town called Matamoros. It was nearly midnight. Dark. Hot. Damp. Eighteen members of my platoon were riding in three separate Bell Huey helicopters. Flying low enough to read road signs and fast enough not to bother.

I scanned the terrain below using the scope on my M16. The

goal was to spot anyone who might be on a rooftop with heavy weaponry. Was I scared? No. Was I lying to myself about not being scared? Yes.

We'd been hunting Diego Correra for three years. I personally had been assigned to six different raids on his drug fields and had been introduced to his legendary "business etiquette" firsthand. Yet I never got the pleasure of introducing him to my M16.

Our helicopters banked left. We were avoiding the city's population. It was a sizable town but not sizable enough that the growl of a chopper would go unnoticed.

The entirety of our intel came from an anonymous source who divulged only a single detail about himself: his name was the Fat Man. We knew nothing else about him. We had no idea if he was a defector from Correra's cartel or if he was the governor of Maine. *Fat Man?* I pictured a bloated, balding car salesman with crusted mustard on his tie, running to pay-phone booths with borrowed quarters to call me.

This morning he gave us the best news we've ever had. "Correra is in Matamoros. Tonight."

Two hours later, we were airborne. I kissed my kids good-bye and tried super hard to seem like a normal mom.

I'm not, though.

There are three main things that can go wrong while jumping out of a helicopter. You could get shot before you jump. You could get shot while actually falling. You could get shot after you complete your fall.

On this mission, we didn't anticipate there would be a fourth thing that could go wrong: your enemy kicks your teeth in.

I had on heat-protective gloves, but I let my boots absorb the majority of the work. I pinched the cord with the arch of one foot against the instep of the other. I don't know how the friction didn't cause a small forest fire, but, honestly, my boots have never shown signs of burn. Credit the US Marine Corps for that. Or me eating salads.

The ground greeted me like a speeding truck. *Wham*. Release, roll, get to position, crouch, aim, hold. Lieutenant Rita Ramirez hit the field second, taking front watch. She was my no-nonsense assistant team leader, so she'd be the caboose once our human caravan got going. Sergeant Kyra Holmes, the best navigator and the best shot, led on point as our sniper. My allies; my two best friends.

I'd never had less intel on a situation, and it was making me an anxious wreck, but my job as colonel was to win the Academy Award for seeming nonwrecked. The shrubbery up ahead was starting to afford us a view as we approached it. I could see the backyard of Diego's compound in front of us.

Showtime.

In general, this hombre used two to three roaming guards even when he was the visitor to a location. I'd have loved to believe these men would be his worst troops: the ones who drew the short straws and had to take the graveyard shift by obligation, the majority of their thoughts on whatever discount porn they might be missing out on.

But that's a dangerous assumption. These could be his best soldiers.

We divided into our three teams: two to engage from the sides and one to come over the back wall. Alpha Team, Bravo Team, Charlie Team.

Rita and I took Alpha toward the driveway.

Quiet and invisible. Those are the golden adjectives. We moved with as much silence as our boots would allow. No scuffling. No talking. Moving along routes that yield as much visual cover as possible. Bracing ourselves for the most complicated phase.

The entry.

Ideally, you fast rope directly onto a target, but Diego had used RPGs in the past: rocket-propelled grenades. So, no, the prospect of hovering in the air like a noisy piñata while angry men with rockets watched you from below was not desirable. Fifteen seconds up there would be an eternity. Too much potentially bad luck involved. No thanks.

My platoon didn't like bad luck. My platoon didn't even like good luck. We preferred drawing up two hundred different football-style diagrams with X's and O's, staring at maps and sketches, and letting everyone verbally shoot holes at our plans until we found one plan that seemed logistically bulletproof.

We passed quietly through the gate. And we arrived in the courtyard.

Already? Wait a second. This breach took no effort.

Oddly, this was the first sign that things were about to go horribly wrong.

The place was fully abandoned. From above, the compound looked like a normal set of buildings, but here at ground level, you could see this interior was hollow. Literally hollow.

Another group had already met us from the far end of their horseshoe-shaped journey. Bravo Team. We were all kind of staring at each other through a very empty structure: just some pillars and an old house with zero furniture.

"Bravo clear," said the Bravo Team Leader from a back room.

My heart sank.

"Charlie clear," said the Charlie Team Leader. Charlie had already arrived from the middle.

Is this over?

"Alpha clear," I said, barely able to hide the disappointment in my voice. I wasn't getting nominated for that Oscar anytime soon.

My platoon quickly began to scour the complex. There was no-body here.

Was the Fat Man lying?

And then Kyra found the first sign of what was to come: Blood. Lots of it.

I was thinking we had just executed the biggest failure ever. I was wrong. The failure was just getting started.

CHAPTER 2

DIEGO CORRERA WAS MUCH more evasive than our mission budgets could handle. Some of our top Pentagon brass said he's just not qualified to be a priority, but during his rise to glory he butchered nearly twenty-nine hundred human beings, most of them innocent citizens, many of whom were children, with the worst aspect being *how* he did it.

It's a process he lovingly calls El Padron.

The first time I saw photos of El Padron, I threw up. I thought I'd seen it all. I'd been on over fifty missions in twelve years and led combat action in five different nation states, but I'd never seen anything as harsh as El Padron. It's like the guy was setting a world record for the most disturbing usage of pliers.

And there in that empty compound in Matamoros, I was about to get my first personal taste of it.

"Fat Man, this is Spider Actual. Do you copy?" I tried my radio on the off-chance that the Fat Man was patched in. "Fat Man, you there?"

He wasn't.

Kyra had blood on her sleeve from brushing up against a dark wall that was absolutely drenched with it. Fresh, bright red.

I began making my way to the roof of Diego's compound.

Something was wrong here. Very wrong. Yes, it's possible that Diego was tipped off ahead of time, but, beyond my annoyance at being evaded, there was a growing unrest in me. How can this place be literally empty?

"Fat Man, do you copy?" I said again as I climbed up the courtyard wall, grabbing a rain gutter to pull myself up to the roof of the compound. My goal was to scout the town from a high position. There would be a decent vantage point up there. I needed to at least "feel" the visual, to satiate my nagging need to see that there was nothing to see.

There atop the second story, I raised my M16 and scoped the horizon with its sight lens. "Fat Man, come in." I was hoping to snoop around whatever was visible a half mile down the main road.

I wouldn't need to look that far.

El Padron.

It was on our front porch.

The "message" was set up for us in front of the compound. At first I saw only one. But then I saw another and another. And by the time Rita joined me, there were twenty-three to behold.

Police officers.

All dead.

Two dozen Matamoros police officers, murdered, left in the street like confetti. Killed for no other reason than to tell us, tell my platoon, who we were dealing with. We were being warned.

"How can you be sure this is for us?" asked Rita.

"It's for us," I said, wishing it weren't.

"Colonel!" yelled Kyra.

She was calling me from below. She was already on the street, investigating. The other platoon members were slowly, quietly elbowing each other, calling attention to the spectacle out front.

Kyra was the first one to the center and she had found something she wanted me to see.

I went down. And I saw.

Each of the dead bodies was mutilated with an extra type of signature. It was known as Diego's Cross. He would etch it into the flesh of his victims. The wounds were fresh, the blood still trickling. His violently sarcastic artwork had taken place just minutes ago.

Minutes ago.

That meant our entire arrival was logged on their evening agenda. I grabbed the radio handset off our radio man. No more audio protocol.

Rita tried to slow me down. "Wait, Colonel." She was going to tell me there's no connection, no listener, no rational reason to bark what I was going to bark. But it didn't matter: I had already begun shouting into the void. "Fat Ass, I swear to God, do you have any idea what's on the street in front of—?"

"Tango, eight o'clock!" Kyra called out, dropping to her knee and aiming her M27 directly at the shadows behind us.

We all instantly spun around, took cover, and aimed, waiting for the silence to usher in a shit storm of trouble.

None of us lit up, though. Our potential tango, as in potential target, as in potential enemy, as in we're about to reduce you to burger meat, was a little girl.

"Hold your fire!" shouted Rita.

"Hold," I reiterated to my platoon. *We're not here to kill kids.* "Hold!"

The child was about nine years old. Unarmed. Alone. A local. She was emaciated but there was a raw energy to her eyes. She was driven by something deep inside.

She stood in the middle of the street and looked right at me, eye to eye. She knew I was in charge and I could tell she would deliver her message only to the one in charge. Undaunted, unabashed, she faced me directly, then raised her index finger and gradually pointed in my direction.

Slowly, viciously, she pointed at her own throat. She made the cross sign.

"*Ya tenemos usted,*" she said with a carnivorous smile.

Then she walked away. Her words hung in the air.

We already have you.

CHAPTER 3

ARRIVING BACK HOME IN Archer, Texas, usually felt good.
It had been only a two-day jaunt, the Matamoros fiasco, but that's
enough to feel like forever.

You miss everything when you're away. Everything. The traffic,
the radio, the mini-malls, even the trash on the street. Why? Because that trash is hometown trash. That trash is made up of
scraps of daily life. My daily life.

But nothing compares to the first glimpse of your front door.
Both of my daughters love Halloween more than they love their
own birthdays, so at this point our porch was covered with
pumpkins and skeletons and Disney witches. Even though it was
mid-September.

They were expecting me tomorrow morning, which technically
was still five hours away, so I didn't want to wake them. I didn't
even want to wake my husband. I just wanted to slide under
the poofy sheets and reverse spoon him. To disappear into his
dreams. True stealth.

He was a heavy sleeper. His fantasy football app would be the
last thing on his phone besides one or two naughty texts from
yours truly. He'd be out cold. Our hallway floor always creaked,
so I took my time with each step. Nothing seems louder than

walking to your kitchen at 2:00 a.m. I could even hear the fabric of my pants slide against itself.

I gently pushed open our bedroom door. We always sleep with it slightly ajar. Tonight was no exception. He'd learned over the years—the years and years of unpredictably long or short missions—that his sexy colonel could potentially saunter in at any hour of the night, and if he played his cards right, he could get that "she outranks me" sex he bragged to his buddies about. Though, on this occasion I was already spent, already shell-shocked from what my platoon had seen. *We already have you.* Drained from a day and a half without sleep. Tonight I'd be using him as a slab of warm comfort. He has his back to me. Curled in a fetal position. Perfect.

I crawled onto the bed.

And then my hand squished into a swamp.

A wet area of the mattress.

My first thought was that our eight-year-old was just here, napping, and probably had wet the bed. She'd probably left, stayed quiet, and thereby Daddy never knew. My second thought was that my husband had a fever and he was sweating out what had become a lagoon.

My third thought wasn't a thought. It was professional opinion. *My husband is dead.*

I finally saw it. Bullet holes through his shoulder and through his temple. Heavy sleeper—they shot him in his dreams. His head was half gone. He'd been dead for at least three hours. *Who's they?* My legs were already carrying me down the hall. It wasn't even an instinct. It was like I was watching myself appear ahead of me. Fast. Inexorable. *Who's they?* Already bursting through their bedroom door. Already flicking up the light switch, already prepared . . .

To scream.

The training manual says to arrive at a violent situation and execute your training with dispassionate precision. Don't yell out your reaction. The enemy could still be nearby. Don't gasp. The enemy could get the first attack.

Don't let anyone know what emotional state you're in.

Keep quiet. Watch exits. Assess the scene. Keep your weapon up.

I did none of that.

My daughters were dead.

Both of them. Within several feet of each other. I grabbed my limp babies. The manual says to flee a situation where there is clear and present danger and insufficient intel. That's Chapter Nine.

What chapter is the chapter that says how to carry your dead daughters over to your dead husband? And place them in front of you, in a futile group hug, so that God could see that he might have made a mistake? That there is an undo button somewhere at his console he can press?

God didn't press it.

Diego's Cross was permanently etched on my family's flesh.

I made the only phone call my hands and my spinal cord were capable of making. I called Rita. I didn't speak. I couldn't. I couldn't make my mouth emit words. But she could hear my throat cracking in the air. She could hear all she needed to hear to know that this isn't Amanda's normal communication. And so Rita was gonna do what Rita would then do.

"This is your home phone?" she asked without expecting a reply. Calm. Decisive. Bankable. "Be there in four minutes."

CHAPTER 4

Present Day

THAT WAS THE BEGINNING. That was what led me here
to this freeway underpass, parked under a tree just beyond it,
eighty miles east of El Paso. A million miles south of paradise.

Waiting. Watching.

I was in a sedan, waiting for the arrival of a particular truck.
Rita was parked five miles away, watching from a small hillside.
Page one of that manual I mentioned earlier says that heat is a
state of mind. You can decide to be uncomfortable. You can decide not. I stopped feeling things entirely. It had been two years
since I became a person without a family. At this point in my life,
my skin doesn't feel. My skin merely assesses.

"Badger Three to Badger Eight."

I was talking to the Fat Man. I was using identification codes
that intentionally misrepresented the size of our team. When
your numbers are small, you want your enemy to think you are
large. When you are large, you want them to think you are small.
So says Sun Tzu.

I was no longer an active Marine. I was freelance.

"How's the road?" asked the Fat Man.

"Empty."

"What about the temperature?"

"Hundred and five," I replied. "About to get hotter."

Rita's voice then came on the radio. "Eyes on tango, Badger Three. Point-eight klicks. Barrel-assin' your way."

I looked up. I saw the truck. A big rig. Unmarked. Driving well over the speed limit, heading toward my position.

Time to rock.

"Good luck," said the Fat Man.

"Don't need it," I told him.

CHAPTER 5

I PUT MY POLICE beacon on the roof of my sedan, flicked on the siren, and stomped on the gas. The enemy was on eighteen wheels and moving fast.

You never know how someone's going to react to getting lit up by the law. Most normal people freeze mentally and pull over erratically slow. They cooperate almost to a fault. But this guy could have warrants out. He could have paperwork issues. He could have a girlfriend who just told him she cheated on his ugly mug. He could have whiskey in him. Brass knuckles. You never knew.

He pulled over as soon he cleared the bend. This picnic was just getting started.

His big rig took a half minute to slow to a stop. I had to assume this was sufficient time for him to radio his contacts, his pals, his boss, his muscle, his mom, whomever. And I, of course, had to assume he was leaning over to his glove box and getting, what would be my guess, a Glock. I had my own Glock. Making for a Glock-on-Glock fight.

I don't like those odds. I don't like a fair fight. Ever. That sort of macho B.S. might work on a TV show, but in real life I never want a level playing field. I want the upper hand in every possible category. If you have a black belt in jujitsu, I want a knife. If you have a knife, I want a gun. If you have a gun, I want a missile. A missile that shoots smaller missiles from its side missiles and that bleeds acid. I want surprise on my side. I want backup. I want a sniper covering my six. I want my enemy drunk, sitting on a toilet, asleep, when I find him.

But that's a perfect story that never gets told in the world of Amanda.

There's always one fun detail that jacks things up a bit.

I was walking up along the left side his trailer. I would have loved to stay in his blind spot but truck mirrors pretty much cover all angles.

I knocked on his door and he opened up. *Game on.*

"Do you know how fast you were going?" I asked him.

"*¿Cómo?*" he replied. Accent thick. Mexican.

"I got you doing eighty-four in a seventy zone." My goal was to keep him off track. Confuse him. Have him think I'm a cop initially.

"*Lo siento pero no hablo Ingles.*" But maybe he was the one confusing me. "*¿Es usted la policía?*"

"Keep your hands where I can see them."

He didn't. His hands were roaming.

"Your *hands.*" I gestured to indicate the obvious.

"*¿Mis manos?*" he asked, seeming to barely, just barely, understand me. "*No hay una problema.*"

He was reaching for his center console. Slowly. As if his slowness would go unnoticed.

"*¡No te muevas!*" I shouted at him. "*Tus manos.*"

"*¿Mis manos?*" Was he really thinking he was going to grab his weapon before I could react? Yes, he was.

Five tenths of a second later, he was pointing a .38 Special in my general direction and I was already firing three quick shots at his hand.

I missed my first but the second and third bullets both nailed him in the arm, ruining his chances for a response.

There was a second guy in the cab, the wingman. I hadn't yet seen him from my vantage point. He was getting ready to join the party, but Rita was lightning-quick to yank open his passenger door and get the muzzle of her Glock on his rib cage.

She had capitalized on the previous distraction.

"Damn, lady, what the hell's your problem?" yelled the injured driver.

"Get out of the cab!" shouted Rita. "Both of you. Now!"

They were slow and grumpy about it, muttering all sorts of hateful gems under their breath. *Bitches. Putas. Lesbians.* Trust me, coming from your enemy, these are all compliments. Every last syllable. The best part is they were cooperating, bless their little cotton socks, they were moving along, hands interlaced behind their sweaty heads, exiting, and separating themselves from our eighteen-wheel trophy.

"You're gonna run down the road," Rita told them. "Directly down the center line. And if you turn your head back...I shoot you."

They started to trot away from us.

"If you run slow, I shoot you," she declared.

They increased the speed of their trot by a billionth of a percent.

Rita fired a shot through the flannel shirt flap of contestant number two. Didn't hit his body. Just hit his shirt. From a field goal away. On a moving target. She's that good.

They started to sprint.

"If you drift to the side, I shoot you!" she yelled.

They ran so dead center it was almost comical. And soon the heat waves from the asphalt drowned them from our sight. And soon we were going to work. Barbecue time!

We had backpacks full of C-4, my favorite way to end the life of a large vehicle. Fuse detonation. Lightweight. Very stable. Rita cracked the padlock off the back with the butt of her gun and swung open the trailer doors. The cargo bay was mostly empty except for a pyramid of sacks piled up against the front end. Sacks of cocaine? Yes. Sacks of meth? Yes.

Sacks of them.

Not a bad haul. I'd say a quarter of a million's worth, as a guess.

Leaving our backpacks nuzzled down in the heart of the matter, fuses lit, we scrambled out of the trailer top-speed. We both got in my car and spun around, fishtailing it, gravel flying, hustling to flee the scene as fast possible, just as—*boom*—a concussion blast of ten M112 bricks of plastique shattered that truck into last Tuesday.

Diego Correra isn't going to like this.

CHAPTER 6

NOR WAS HE gonna like this . . . .

Within a twenty-mile drive from the previous raid, we had located the second of Correra's big rigs. A Peterbilt. We were tracking the driver on a desolate stretch of Highway 285, waiting for him to be truly alone. The question was whether or not he had been warned by the last guy.

He pulled over as soon as he saw my police beacon light up.

As far as we knew, the last thing his buddy would've announced is that some asshole cops were detaining him. We made sure they didn't take their phones with them on their involuntary hike. So, yes, they might have broadcasted that the law was stopping them but, fine, that was a much better bulletin than, *Dios mío, some crazy bitches just blew up our truck.*

When we got the Peterbilt driver to open his driver door, he was more angry than surprised. Almost indignant.

"Do you know whose shit this is?"

I looked over at Rita. He was engaging us as if we were bribed cops, as if we were on Diego's payroll. What do we say to this? Play it cool? Play dumb? We didn't look like cops. At best, we looked like immigration patrol. But this was the type of bandit who wouldn't care regardless.

"Do you know whose shit this is!" he asked again.

"I guess it's mine." I had to speak up. My mouth does that. And then it added, "As of today."

"This is the property of Diego Correra, you dead pig. You know who you're dealing with?"

"Not really. Is he nice? He seems nice. Does he give you dental benefits? Because you could use some."

"And you just wasted your time," he said, pointing to his trailer, "because this shit is empty." He started laughing, his yellow teeth gleaming in the sun. "I already made the drop."

Rita and I traded a look. This would really suck. An empty bed. It would mean Diego had one-upped me. Again. The driver seemed excited that we were escorting him to the rear of his vehicle, that we were about to open up his trailer's doors and witness his hilarious joke.

"Open the gate," Rita said to him. *"¡Muévelo!"*

He led us to the back and started to unlatch the door. Squeaking the bolt like crazy. The pride in this guy's demeanor—I was cringing at the thought that his truck would be bare.

The door opened up and, here we go, two of his pals were right there, AK-47s all set, immediately unleashing a spray of bullets right at us. *Ambush!*

Rita and I both dove for the ground, tumbling as tightly as we could, to roll forward, into the protective cover of the truck itself. Wheels, metal, axles, anything. My only thought was to get behind a barrier, any possible barrier, because if these guys had the sense to shoot directly downward through their floor, they'd have a good chance of shredding us.

And I hate chances like that.

I was just getting to a crouch and soon enough a rain of high-caliber bullets came streaking down around us. Rita was on the far side of the combat zone, already in the ditch, just off the road, scurrying for some rocks. Smart *muchacha*. She would have a great angle of attack once they emerged from the tailgate.

The thing is, now all three of them were armed.

I was listening to their footsteps above me. They had emptied out their magazines on us and a reload might give me just enough time to roll out from the wheel well and unleash one mediocre flurry of upward shots. Glocks versus AK-47s. Not fun. Never bring a slingshot to a missile fight. The creaking floor above indicated my enemy was doing the same thing I was. Positioning. The driver stayed still, I think, but his two pals headed toward the exit. He must be staying home to guard the goods. Or to come over to where I was, by the wheels. I let loose three quick shots. Fifteen degrees apart.

I heard him gasp.

Payday. I must have at least nicked him. The other two guys started whispering to each other. I think they were deciding to leap out and surprise me because what happened next was a one-woman greeting party by my favorite lieutenant.

Rita took them out from her hiding place in the ditch. Two quick shots. And two quick dropped bodies.

"Two out!" she yelled.

"Trailer!" I yelled back. She needed to know we had a third of our enemy still on the menu.

"*Compadre,*" she shouted to the third guy. "We have you trapped! Throw the gun out! Then come slowly into my sight!"

I could hear him shuffling around. I must have grazed him in the leg or something nonvital. He had strength and energy. I could hear him prepping for his epic finish.

"Last chance!" I shouted. "Or we're gonna blow your ass to burger meat."

"*Ultima vez!*" shouted Rita. "*Tenemos plastique.*"

She was hoping the threat of our explosives would convince him to behave. We made our decent offer. Would he take it?

A tiny moment of silence settled over the desert. We were alone. Possibly for miles. A slight breeze came and went. Then suddenly a storm of bullets squirted out of the trailer's side wall. The guy was probably praying he could somehow hit Rita without knowing where she was.

I shoved my second bag of C-4 directly into the belly of the trailer. Rita dashed up and tucked her own bag near the trailer hitch. Because we couldn't operate directly on the interior of the target, we'd have to compensate by doubling our dose on the exterior.

This guy was about to be erased from earth.

"Fuse!" I yelled.

"Fuse!" she yelled back. We couldn't see each other but this wasn't our first rodeo: We knew our standard operating procedure was to default to detonation. "Three...Two...One..."

I lit my fuse. She lit hers.

We both ran for the opposite side of the highway. Toward the parallel ditch on the far side. Diving for cover. Just as our friend let out another spray of bullets through the wrong wall of his mobile fort. Within five seconds, *wham!* Our explosives lit up half of west Texas. A towering fireball.

Police sirens had already started to wail in the distance, so we had to go.

The law was coming.

And we weren't exactly on the right side of it.

CHAPTER 7

KYRA JOINED US FOR the next raid. She had missed the last two because we'd sent her to obtain more explosives on the black market. It sounds funny to say, but we ran out of things that go *boom*. She was waiting on her connection, a shady group of bikers in Lovington, New Mexico, while Rita and I executed those first two raids. C-4 is only about fifteen dollars a pound. But that's the price only if you have time to wait and if you trust your source and if you need only a small quantity and if you don't need to be an anonymous buyer.

We were absolutely none of those things.

The bikers wanted five thousand dollars.

Nobody said justice was cheap.

During the next two days, the three of us converged on every active Correra shipment in Texas. He had routes strewn all over the back roads of El Paso, Dallas, Houston, and Laredo. Some loads were obviously his. Like the unmarked Peterbilt with serial numbers still visible for us to confirm. Some were tricky. He had a six-wheeler disguised as a Hertz rental truck, upon which his goons even went so far as to latch a bicycle on the back, just to throw off us dogs completely.

But we had the list from the Fat Man. And the list was relentlessly accurate. It gave the description of each shipment and a time frame of when it would pass a certain point. "Highway 87. Milepost 55. Tuesday evening. White big rig with blue cab."

We blew it all up like clockwork.

The quantity of C-4 Kyra obtained was phenomenal. More powerful than we expected. Sent a tower of fire and smoke high up into the clouds.

We were perched on a plateau overlooking a nice lonely stretch of Interstate 380. Kyra was using her Steiner high-power binoculars to track our prey.

"Well, I have him in sight," said Kyra. "But . . ."

"But what?" I asked.

"Cessna. Five o'clock."

Cessna? I looked up in the expansive desert sky. Yup. I saw a small plane circling our general area. Was it state troopers? Sheriffs? This was a problem. The police were using planes now. We had detonated enough C-4 to make national news. Nobody knew that we were the ones behind these raids, which was ideal, but the fact that there were drugs in the trucks was kept secret from almost every single article. To discourage copycat behavior, the authorities didn't want to report moral victories. Fine. I didn't want applause. I wanted Diego. But I called off our half-week rampage at target number seven.

"We're letting this one go," I said.

"Because of the plane?" she replied.

"Too much attention."

"Let's just do this one last one. We're right here."

"Negative, Sergeant. Stand down."

We had earned our rest. It was time to lie low for a bit and be as normal as possible. Diego Correra operates nearly fifteen shipments a month. We hit half of them and thereby pissed in his revenue stream to the tune of four million dissolved dollars. For men who like money, the best way to hurt them is to punch them in the money.

And I was just getting started.

CHAPTER 8

THE PLACE WE WERE heading home to was Righteous. Literally. Righteous was the name of the repair garage that Kyra and I built. She started it when neighbors kept asking her to tweak their motorbikes and lawn mowers and dune buggies. Eventually, she graduated herself to cars and trucks and even boats. All of us were comfortable with power tools. Kyra, however, was a mechanical genius. And in a town like Archer, Texas, where locals thrive on old motors, we had stumbled on the formula for contentment.

For me, going in on Kyra's repair business was simply a chance to keep my hands busy, which was a chance to keep my brain busy, which was a chance to keep my heart busy.

Not that it ever worked.

Not that I could ever find sixty consecutive seconds in a day when I wasn't thinking about my family.

Next door to Righteous the Repair Shop was Righteous the Cafe. We served miserably underpriced doughnuts and delicious everything else. On Tuesdays Rita made gumbo. Fresh sausage. Fresh veggies. Some of the locals would bring in produce from their own gardens.

It was that kind of town.

Rita and her husband had made quite a nest for themselves. The income from the cafe wasn't gluttonous but it was enough to cover its own cost. And its ten-acre setup was perfect for our needs. Base camp.

That night I was helping in the back with the dishes when Rita came to me with the mail.

"I think you should see this," she said.

It was a greasy, plain envelope addressed to me. The smudges made it look like it came from another mechanic somewhere. Clever camouflage. But it was a little too greasy. A little too carefully messed up. I knew the situation. We all did. I started to open it, with Rita giddy, as Kyra locked the door. Inside was a check for two hundred thousand dollars.

The Fat Man delivereth.

He may be a lot of things (annoying, tardy, elusive, cryptic, suspicious, allegedly fat) but one thing is unmistakable about our unknown friend: He pays.

He pays well.

Two hundred thousand dollars split into three goes a long way in a backwater town like Archer. None of us lived like royalty. We were more likely to wear Smith & Wesson than Dolce & Gabbana. We never took vacations. We never bought yachts.

Kyra held up the check for us like a title belt. We all smiled at each other knowing we did good work. For me, my share, it was sixty-six thousand dollars that simply went into a bank. Just a testament to the fact that money couldn't buy back a dead husband or two kids.

It couldn't even buy the end of Diego Correra.

Or could it?

CHAPTER 9

THAT NIGHT, TO CELEBRATE the dent we put in Correra's financial shinbone, we opened up the cafe for a late-night romp. Open to the whole neighborhood. Music. Pie. Beer. On the house. We were that kind of town.

We cleaned up the garage and annexed it off as the world's most backwoods discotheque. Picture the barn dance in *Footloose* minus the barn. Domestic beer flowing. Free biscuits and gravy. Braised pork ribs worth starving yourself all day for. And, my goodness, a slice of pecan pie à la mode.

Rita and her rhythmic hubby captivated the middle of the dance floor. Kyra was getting hit on by half the locals, and I . . .

I couldn't be happier watching from the sidelines.

I managed to sneak back toward the periphery, unseen by the crowd. I didn't want to draw attention. There's a type of loneliness where you're just aching to be approached by someone to coax you back into the crowd. Then there's the loneliness that can't be solved by the mechanisms of this world.

I have that second type.

I miss my husband so much. I look up at the stars every night and search for his soul. I know he's there. I can feel it. I can hear him talking to me. And I know he's got both our little cherubs with him. And they're all pleasantly restless, waiting for me. But they're also looking down with understanding.

At least, I hope so.

I have the same argument in my head over and over. That I blew it. That I got them killed. That no matter what I do to Diego, it'll never address what Diego did to us.

Then I hear my family chime in. I hear them tell me I've always stood on the right side of any decision in life. That I'm not perfect. I make mistakes. But I don't make mistakes out of selfishness. I'm trying as hard as I can to contribute to this world.

To protect the kids of future generations.

"What are you doing?" came a voice from behind.

It was Gus, the honorary vice mayor. We have an honorary vice mayor. It's that kind of town. Gus was ninety-seven years old and didn't look a day over ninety-six. Still drove a car. Still mowed his own lawn. He saw me out there in the darkness, beyond the doorway to the dance-hall garage.

"Oh…I…uh…heard a couple coyotes," I replied. "And wanted to make sure the hens were okay in the coop."

"Always on recon."

"Me? No. I'm just secretly a terrible dancer. I can't let anyone witness that."

He offered his hand. "Well, now I have to expose you." Bouncing his head to the music, he wanted to see me Texas two-step. No human being should be subjected to the sight of me dancing.

But he insisted. "You're a good person, Colonel. You deserve to wear a smile tonight."

He knew what was going on with me. I think the entire town did. When we entered the room and headed for the dance floor, they all cheered like I was a hero. It was really embarrassing, and it made me feel stupid. But I swear I could hear my kids cheering in the background as well.

And I could hear my husband's voice. I could hear him warning me.

That things were about to get rough.

CHAPTER 10

AROUND HERE IT DOESN'T take much to stick out. Archer, Texas. If all you did was get a faulty haircut, everyone would know about it within a half day. And it would be talked about. Passionately.

So when he arrived, of course he was the main topic of gossip.

I started hearing rumors that there was a stranger asking questions at local businesses, trying to seem casual about it. It raised red flags with certain friends of mine. We didn't know this stranger's name yet, but already the gaggle of ladies down at the salon were making uneducated guesses:

"I bet his name is Lorenzo. He's tall. Like Lorenzo tall."

"No, no, no, he's a Victor," said the second lady. "Those yummy shoulders."

"You're both wrong about my Derek," said the third lady.

It probably wasn't Derek. Most locals thought he was at least half Latino. He reportedly had a very slight but definite accent while doling out random questions to random people about the neighborhood. *Is it safe around here? Would this be a good place to raise a family? How well do you know your neighbors?*

He apparently had been asking around town about us without actually asking around town about us. Until the next day when he decided to stop being coy. He marched right into Righteous the Cafe and was soon joking around with the busboy and suckering him into a free round of billiards on our pool table. Kyra didn't like that. She didn't like that he skimped on paying the measly seventy-five cents for a rack.

"Excuse me, pal," she said to him. "Games ain't quite free."

But he wasn't going down easy. In fact, he wasn't even going to participate in the same conversation she started.

"So whose bar is this?" he asked.

"Bar?" said Kyra.

"Bar . . . cafe . . . I like it. You built this place yourself?" He smiled with each sentence. He had that Ted Bundy sort of charm. You couldn't help but like him, but you were also pretty sure he'd be murdering you by 9:00 p.m.

Kyra was direct. "It belongs to Rita. Me and Coll run the auto shop."

"Coll?" he asked, racking up the table for eight-ball. "Amanda Collins?"

"Are you here to play or to gossip? Because I can get some yarn and we can sit and knit. Otherwise, seventy-five cents."

He gestured to a dollar bill that was already on the table. He had indulged her fee. Without her knowing. Sly. Hot-guy sly.

She took the money as he cracked a thunderbolt break and sent three balls in three different pockets. All solids. He was here to play. In every sense of the word.

I was hearing all this firsthand. I was in the back of the diner, carrying boxes to the kitchen, shielding my face from view by my stack of cardboard. He hadn't seen me.

Until now.

Until he turned to me, calmly, knowing I was there the whole time. A cocky smile already orchestrated on his face, as if he knew I was stepping forward, as if his entire mission was this moment.

"Are you Amanda Collins?" he asked me.

Screw this guy.

"I'm not very good at pool," I replied. "So I'll make you a deal."

I set my boxes down and approached his table. "You win: I'll introduce myself. I win: you leave town immediately."

"Ouch. No kiss?"

"Deal?"

I figured I could at least scrimmage with him for a little bit and let him divulge whatever he might divulge about himself.

"Deal." He gave me a dangerously confident nod.

I've seen how these Mexican cartels send a message. When they have a true enemy, like myself, they can't just kill her. They need to make her front-page news.

"Whoops," he said, nailing his next shot nonchalantly. A combo.

How would they kill me? How would they amplify it? A severed head in front of a school? A burned body?

After two more shots, he finally missed, perhaps on purpose, and handed me the cue.

I yanked it from him, noting he had a large pistol in his jacket pocket. He was doing his best to hide this fact from me, but over the years I've gotten disturbingly good at spotting a concealed weapon, even under a puffy jacket.

I've also gotten disturbingly good at a two-cushion corner pocket shot. I kept up with his sharp shooting. We traded two rounds, then I sunk three stripes in a row and positioned myself for an easy fourth. He was better than me, but he was letting me win.

"Eight ball. Side pocket." I said. And sunk it. Game over.

"Good shot, Colonel."

I walked over to the front door, opened it, and held it there for him. "You a man of your word?"

"I am." He slowly walked over to me and stopped to get close to my face. "But I should tell you something."

"Oh yeah?"

"I'm coming back." He walked out the door. Heading to his car. And without looking at me, he added, "With friends."

CHAPTER 11

I DIDN'T SLEEP MUCH that night. I'm a bad sleeper in general, but that night I was staring at the ceiling fan, watching it go in circles, wasting brain cells ruminating on the fact that the blades keep slicing the same area, the same invisible circle of air, never slicing anything new, never improving their position.

I was also listening.

For him. The stranger.

By the time I finally felt slumber take hold of my thoughts, the first light of dawn was piercing my window. I slept like I was dead for an hour or so then awoke again. It was seven o' clock. I was still in bed but my mind was twisting around. Something didn't seem right. And after a half minute I realized what it was. There was no noise from the cafe kitchen.

I generally hear the assistant cooks start banging around early in the morning. Today there were some sounds from out back, but as I lay there, piecing together a sleepy recollection of the early morning hours, I realized the sounds I'd heard came from the garage, not the cafe.

The garage? Uh-oh.

I grabbed my bowie knife and headed outside to check around.

This couldn't be what the Ted Bundy guy meant, could it? This quick of a return?

I crept into the garage through the backdoor and braced myself for the worst.

I didn't click on the light yet. I could see bad news the moment I stepped in. Our stuff was thrown everywhere, strewn all over the ground. The tool chests tipped over. The shelves ransacked. Everything we owned was flipped on its head.

Were they searching for something? What?

While I was standing there, mulling it over, I saw a shadow begin to creep along the wall. Someone prowling.

They were still in the room! The intruders. Whoever they were.

I ducked down behind the fender of a Chevy Tahoe and readied my knife. Terrified. Bewildered. Ready to rock.

Within seconds, I saw my enemy walking past me, well unaware of my presence. He was wearing a dark jacket and a dark hood. Six two. Probably 210 pounds. Up to no good.

I sneaked up on his backside, quick as a house cat, and instantly put him in a choke hold with the blade of my knife pressed directly onto his jugular. Checkmate, son! I had him at an absolute surrender position.

Finally in control, I was ready to ask him three brief questions, almost praying for him to give me false answers so I could have the moral green light to slit his jugular and drain him right on the spot.

And I was all set to begin question number one.

"Who—?"

But just as my mouth began to blurt out the first word, I felt the barrel of a Beretta M9 press on the base of my neck.

"Don't do it, Colonel."

It was the calm voice of my billiard opponent. He was so close I could smell his nuclear-grade aftershave. I wished I had moved more quickly and positioned myself closer to the door so that my flank wouldn't have been so vulnerable, but—damn it—shitty strategy on my part, I was cornered.

And outnumbered.

He did indeed bring his friends. In addition to the thug under my knife, there were now two other thugs standing on both sides of me. In business suits.

I cooperated. I slowly, meekly, lowered my blade away from the throat in question.

"Who are you?" I asked him through gritted teeth.

"My name is Warren Wright," he said. "And these are my friends. We work for a fun little group called the DEA."

CHAPTER 12

AGENT WARREN WRIGHT HOLSTERED his weapon. All the guys around me then seemed to relax a bit. A very small bit. With the cat out of the bag, the fact that he'd revealed himself to me as a fed, the fact that they're *all* feds, the fact that his boring name is Warren Wright, the entire group seemed to decide I was no longer a threat to them.

Pfffff. If they only knew…

How close I came to breaking his jaw regardless. Him, with his stupid suit. And his stupid hair. And his impossibly white teeth. What they were doing here in my garage had yet to be politely explained to me. So I was impolitely furious.

Warren looked me up and down. He was smirking. He had enjoyed his words in this situation. He had enjoyed every last syllable.

"You look old up close," I told him.

"Incorrect. I look handsome. And responsible. But most of all you know what I look like? I look like the one who isn't going to jail."

"Jail," I repeated with disdain.

"Would you like me to tell you why?"

"Nope."

"Would you like me to tell you how done you are?"

"Nope."

"I wonder…have you heard anything about big rigs blowing up? On routes out of small towns? Small Texas border towns?"

I didn't have an answer for that. I didn't want to try to deny it. He obviously knew. He had half his department standing there, crammed into my Podunk garage. They weren't here for a banjo lesson, that's for sure.

"Let me repeat myself, Colonel Amanda Rae Collins, Highly Decorated Employee of the Month, have you heard anything about big rigs getting blown up?"

"N—"

"No, you haven't," he said, cutting off my *no* with his own slightly more contrived *no,* then pausing. This was him setting up his corny crescendo. (God, these government jackoffs are all the same. As if they were all issued the identical dismal sense of humor at academy graduation. The type of idiot banter that guarantees they will never have sex.) All to set up his grand explanation of world facts: "You know why you haven't heard about it? Because *we* buried the story," he replied to himself, with pride. "*We* did."

Silence.

I think it was my turn to speak. To be impressed.

"Each time?" I finally broke the silence.

"We can do that."

"Do you want me to clap? Slowly?"

Warren leaned in close. I could smell the federal on his breath. The faint odor of decaf and bureaucracy. "We're watching you and your little girlfriends. We know all about your history with Diego. The games. The felonies."

"He's more than a *felon.*"

"'I'm talking about *you.* About illegal behavior."

"Oh, yes, please keep *talking*. Let's just spend the next month *talking*. And filling out forms. And holding conference calls. And spell-checking email. Meanwhile, that bag of shit is still at large. And have you seen what he's done?"

"I've seen what *you've* done," said Warren. "So far. And I'll tell you something, we know how to *keep* you doing it."

"What?"

He didn't answer.

There's no way he could be saying what I thought he was saying—was he giving us his government-issued blessing to continue our crusade? "Keep me doing what?" I asked again.

He had turned away and was about to exit the garage but he stopped. This was his patented move. He was going to savor this moment.

"Doing...nothing," he said.

I had to stand there for a moment and absorb it. *Keep me doing nothing? How could he think we weren't accomplishing anything!?* He looked over at me, smug about his little zinger. Then he nodded for his nerd clan to pick up a few items of mine: to gather two of our trunks and a couple of our duffel bags, holding our only six rifles, plus our only stash of ammo.

"That's our only chance!" I protested, referring to the weapons. "That gear was *not* easy to get, you need to leave all that here."

"Sure, Amanda, as soon as you show me a permit." His posse then funneled behind him as he exited. *"Hasta luego."*

I watched him leave. (More like smelled him leave.) I was fuming. "Oh, the *luego* is coming, you bastard. Just you wait."

CHAPTER 13

CHURCH WAS FULL ON Sunday. Church is always full in Archer. Part of it is pure piety. Part of it is Rita. Rita is one of the most beautiful souls this town has ever seen. One of the most eloquent. One of the most loved. Our pride and joy. Our pastor.

She was mid-sermon. And reiterating one particular point over and over again. "I'm so sorry," she said to the congregation.

She was talking about the DEA raids. Most everyone knew about them at this point, but she took them personally. She took them as an affront to her way of life.

"... That they would come into your neighborhoods, violating the sanctuary of the Home. That they would trample the rights and values of the very backbone of this proud community, the fundamental backbone: family."

A murmur of *amens* circulated in the room. About four hundred people were present, and aside from maybe two or three teenagers texting each other and Gus snoring gently, I daresay every single sheep in this flock was fully invested.

"I'm so sorry that our *families* were subjected to this," said Rita. "It's no secret that my busy past has drawn undue attention to you, and I beg you your forgiveness." Another murmur of support from the crowd.

My thoughts couldn't help wandering to the last remark from Agent Warren Wright. *Nothing.* Uttered merely days ago. *Amanda is doing nothing.* It wasn't the caustic attitude behind it that stung me: It was the truth of it.

I had indeed done nothing.

I had accomplished nothing. I had improved nothing. Diego was probably richer and smiling harder today than he had ever smiled before. All thanks to me and my big bucket of nothing.

Kyra was in the back. She didn't (as she put it) "subscribe to all this stuff." But she'd do anything to support one of our trio, even if it meant enduring two hours of (as she put it) "doctrine." Secretly, I was hoping one of the nice guys from the fire department in the third row would turn around and ask her to, I don't know, roller skate with him, or something. But Rita was too captivating up front.

It was poetic and inspiring. And I was so caught up in it, her quotes from the Good Book, the way she ushered us into hymnals, that it took me a few seconds to realize she was about to shatter my Sunday morning.

"Amanda, would you do us the honors?" she said.

What?

She was looking at me. Me? Honors? What? Why was she suddenly mentioning my name in the middle of the sermon?

Rita had just asked me, in front of everyone, to come up and share my views on "hope." She had asked me about it yesterday. But I thought she meant to write my dumb thoughts on someone's greeting card or something. I had no idea she was going to make me say it out loud in front of hundreds of people.

The entire church turned to look at me sitting there. I swear an entire minute passed. I was stunned. Gus soon leaned over and whispered to me, "She wants you to go up front." I guess he wasn't asleep after all.

Um.

I started to make my way to the front of the room.

There were warm nods from various townspeople. Dentists. Moms. Dads. Janitors. The wondrous slice of diverse American pie that any serving of Texas can offer. And, good gosh, they were all expecting me to say something amazing.

I slowly made my way to the front. I have spoken quite often to large groups, to my troops, but I did so as a colonel. I'd stood on platforms under a large military tent. I commanded the Fifth Regiment. As a *colonel.* That's 1,227 Marines under my assignment, allowing me to design their life or death struggles.

I got to the altar.

I'm not a colonel these days.

Rita held me in place for a moment. I dread this stuff. Seriously dread it. "We all know about so much of Amanda's efforts out in the field," she said to the crowd. "But what most of us don't get to see is how much courage she displays in her day-to-day affairs."

Oh, my God.

"She is determined," continued Rita. "She gives 100 percent."

Oh, my God. We all get through our day, whatever that day may bring. We all face it. We all battle it. I'm not special. The room was spinning. I hated standing up there. Rita finally finished and gave me a nod along with a graceful gesture that the podium was now mine.

When I talk to troops I'm not Amanda. I'm a colonel. And that colonel got sealed in an imaginary envelope when my husband died. I didn't have her inside me anymore. She was gone. So I was capable only of being 100 percent regular me at that point. And as I looked out at the sea of expectant faces, regular me freaked out.

I glanced over at Rita, who remained at my flank, the perfect position for an assassination. She smiled warmly, having no clue that she was setting me up for pure failure.

I mustered all my courage and conviction and emitted the following.

"...Uh..."

And that stupid-ass syllable, amped by the church's brand new 110-decibel sound system installed by gleeful Kyra, sounded like the belch of a dragon.

My hands started to shake.

"...Um...The...R-Rita...She wanted me to say a few words about taking a...Taking a...s-stand."

Good Lord, that sentence was the worst thing that ever came out of my mouth.

"Taking a stand...is...is hard."

My breath was gone. I could hear my voice quiver. Some people started to shift around in their seats.

"But it's only hard when you forget the one thing that matters most," I said. "The people you're standing up for."

There. I managed to get one thought out. It was a cliché at best, but at least it almost seemed like a decent point to make.

Looking out at all those eyes looking back at me, I was so far in over my head that I decided, *Screw it*.

Rita's face froze as she saw the look on my face. She was thinking I was about to implode.

I wasn't. I was finding my stride. I was starting to make sense to myself. Not easy to do.

"See, I've faced the working end of a Kalashnikov," I continued, "stepped over Syrian land mines, been trapped in a collapsing bunker in Korea. But I've managed to find hope even in the most hopeless nightmares thanks to one thing: I always knew that I was doing it for my people. Without that thought, I definitely would have tumbled."

I felt like I was making sense to them. The congregation. I paused, feeling the room.

"You brought this on us," came an angry voice from the back.

Which was the last thing in the world I expected to hear. It was this guy who worked at the local dive bar. Phillip, I think was his name. A decent man. Vocal.

"You know we just like to mind our own business here," he continued. "This town doesn't need to go kickin' on a foreign hornet's nest."

A lot of the congregation instantly rallied in my defense. "Amanda is amazing." "Quiet, Phil!" "Don't say stuff like that!"

Phillip continued. "We got our own problems. Vandals. Gangs. Shootings."

"Sit down, Phil!" said a number of people. "You're out of line!"

But I disagreed with their disagreement. I was hearing my own words, echoing in my ears, realizing how hypocritical I'd be to ignore the truth.

"He's right," I said, and the room suddenly quieted. "Phillip's right. I have no business making this town a second priority."

I thanked the crowd and walked back to the pews. Amid silence. It was awkward, no question. But I had figured something out. Phil had helped me see it: I can't just attack Diego and watch him attack me and my people back, us attacking each other back and forth, again and again like the two of us were in a boxing match.

I don't care what the excuses are at this point; I have to finish him.

CHAPTER 14

HOW DO YOU FIGHT a war without weapons? Answer: You don't. The first battle is to prepare for the battle. Which means we needed to get *new* weapons.

DEA interference was just a bump in the road. I couldn't whimper in the corner about how tough I had it. I needed to move forward. I needed to treat every phase of the preparation like it was part of the grand battle.

We'd been fighting with low-budget guns on both sides of the equation, but it was a guarantee that Diego would refortify his drivers immediately—as in, he'd increase their fire power. I could imagine he'd also add secondary vehicles as escorts, maybe a guy on a dirt bike, maybe a guy in a sport pickup, a technical.

Rita found a headline on a Mexico City news site that gnawed at my soul. "Nineteen People Dead in Ranchita." Diego had retaliated against us. Against me. He was ravaging small villages in Mexico that had shown support for US intervention in the past.

"And look at this second article," said Rita. She knew this would get my attention. This update was even worse: The people who were killed were kids. Nineteen girls from an all-girls kindergarten.

My hands were shaking. I was ready to fight the entire planet at this point. I was so sick of hearing about psychotic dickheads doing mass damage, I had to make a move. *We* had to make a move.

The biggest gun store in Archer was run by two brothers from Arkansas. Arm & Arm Gun Depot. In addition to overcharging for every item in the store and boozing on the shooting range, these gentlemen had both been convicted of assault on a disabled kid. Truly not the pride of Archer, they would sell weapons to minors and violate just about every law invented, given the chance.

Which meant Rita, Kyra, and I felt comfortable obtaining weapons from them in our own special way.

It was 2:15 a.m. We were on the outskirts of town, standing in front of Arm & Arm.

"We should make sure—"

Smash!

Before Rita could even finish her brilliant sentence on the importance of being subtle, Kyra sailed a brick through the front window. She was already entering the premises.

"My gosh, our fingerprints will be all over," said Rita. "There's gonna be video. Surveillance."

"No, there won't," I told her.

"How do you know?"

"Because we're gonna burn it down."

CHAPTER 15

WE ENTERED ARM & ARM Gun Depot and ransacked every nook, obtaining the key weaponry we needed for our quest. If you want a short-muzzle compact machine with kick, may I suggest the MP5, easily modified to automatic fire? Picture Tom Cruise running around in *Mission: Impossible*. Now add my face and subtract his cinematic grin. I rarely grin while blasting up a warehouse.

That's the MP5. I love it. And Kyra knows I love it. So we got two.

Rita took a shotgun, double barrel, eight concussion grenades, and an Eickhorn combat knife. Those blades are nasty. You can cut the base of a streetlamp with one. (If you're ever sitting around feeling super angry at streetlamps, I guess).

Kyra started the ignition on our getaway minivan. We had doused the place with gasoline, added some sloppiness so it didn't look like the handiwork of the three most obvious bitches in town and, *whoomf,* we set the place ablaze—

Just as Kyra ran back inside.

What was she doing?! We tried to grab her but she squirmed out of our clutches, disappeared through the door, and, within seconds, emerged toting an SR-25 sniper rifle.

"Christmas in July!" she said.

"It's December," said Rita.

"I know, but nobody says Christmas in December."

CHAPTER 16

A FEW DAYS LATER, we were standing across the street from La Sombre Fashion Boutique, a fancy dress shop in town, at 1:45 a.m. We had been debating which unlucky spot would be our decoy, and this was it. When you're doing multiple break-ins, you have to confuse the pattern a bit, just in case a bunch of sheriffs were in front of a wall map of Texas, putting colored thumbtacks in all the right places.

But something about it felt so odd.

"Are you sure?" asked Rita.

"Based on your wedding dress alone, definitely!" said Kyra. "They so overcharged you."

"It was French," I chimed in.

"I love that dress," said Rita. "I thought you did, too."

"There's no decent reason to charge a good Texas woman fifty-five hundred dollars for a dress!" said Kyra, hurling a brick as hard as she could, shattering the display window. Helluva shot from this far away. She was a pitcher in high school. Never lost the arm.

Within a split second the security alarm was ringing. A fancy-pants French boutique like this has pricey merchandise, so of course the only two patrol cars active this late in a town this small would soon be screeching to a halt right here. Which was our goal.

Because we were leaving.

Our first stop was the Shooter Rooter gun store located on the opposite side of town. We took side streets and drove there as fast as we could.

Skidding to a stop just at the curb, we jumped out and doused the exterior walls with gasoline with the intention to then pour as much as we could down the pipes on the roof. Inner and outer fuel.

This wasn't a necessary part of the Diego equation, but it was important to all three of us. Automatic weapons were in the wrong hands. True, the rights to defend yourself and protect your home are a vital aspect of individual, self-preserving freedoms. But the stores here in Archer had become like video game centers. Kids were coming in, bypassing paperwork, and walking out with hollow points and Armalite assault rifles. Worse, there was a growing armada of teen delinquency in town. Being a known drug stop had proliferated the usage of weaponry to solve problems. We were infested.

"Flame set!" yelled Kyra.

She was on the roof and ready to drop her pilot lighter down the pipe shaft at the same time that Rita and I were going to ignite the outside fuel. This would give us a solid chance of burning the whole thing down at once rather than some sort of half-assed beginners-grade arson.

Flick.

We ran top speed back to the car. Within moments the flames were licking up the sides of the walls.

The bonus of blazing up a gun store is the aid of all the explosives inside that are destined to go off. Heat and pressure can do that.

When it finally exploded, it was like the Fourth of July. In December.

I hated that we were committing arson, but here's what I hated more: junior high school kids getting shot by junior high school kids. So, yeah, when it comes to the lesser of two evils, I'll take this, with a cinematic grin.

CHAPTER 17

THE NEXT MORNING I woke up at 6:05 when my phone began to ring. You'd think there might be a congratulatory message for a righteous deed or two, not that I was looking for one. I couldn't really expect one without the obvious accompanying criminal charge. But the call was from a phone number I didn't recognize, with an area code that seemed two digits short.

"—Grrehhhfffolllll," I said.

When a call wakes me up in the morning, my top goal is to appear completely awake. However, my unstretched vocal cords could do nothing but roar a hello that, I swear, must've sounded like a motorcycle rev.

Didn't matter, though. Within two syllables of my caller's reply I already knew the beginning, middle, and end of what would be the ugliest conversation I'd had in quite some time.

"Amanda," said the man.

It was the voice of disappointment. He wasn't greeting me. He wasn't commending me. He was shaking his head, slowly, side to side at the other end of the phone. I could hear the muscles in his neck.

I was waiting for the tongue click sound of disappointment my mother invented long ago but he plunged ahead.

"Arson? Really?" he said.

This was the Fat Man. The one and only.

"You! You got some nerve," I replied. "I had my balls busted by the feds. *Feds*. Who ransacked my garage, stole my gear, and shat on my morality. And you . . . you didn't do a single thing to help us out. Nope. Meanwhile, the only word I get on Diego Correra—remember him?—is when he gets a PR parade on the evening news!"

He didn't respond. He sat on the silence for a moment.

"You're wasting your time," he finally said. "I need you ready for Diego."

No pause from me. "Listen, Fat Boy, my entire life is dedicated to ending his but I can't do *an-y-thing* with the DEA parking a car in my ass. They came to my town. My town! And they pissed all over it with paperwork from some oily loser named Warren Wright. How am I supposed to take down Diego with all this shit? I need to hit him *directly*, not just his shipments!" I was yelling now. I wasn't even mad. I was more jilted, jilted that the Fat Man hadn't called me sooner. I felt like a high-school cheerleader nagging her ex.

"Colonel Collins, I'm gonna do you a massive favor and pretend you didn't just cry about how hard the DEA is being on you. Are they firing bullets? No. Are they torturing villagers? No. Are they locking you up in a cellar? No. Stay focused."

"Listen, the last time I—"

Click. He was gone.

I hated this guy.

He paid. That's about it. That's about the nicest thing I can say about a gopher hole like him. His checkbook didn't suck.

The thing that scared me, though, all jokes aside, is the fact that my own contact didn't know what the DEA was up to. How is that logistically possible? How could they come after me and my friends without scuffling up a dust storm in Washington? What were they doing in my town? Were they still here?

Were they being bribed by Diego?

Were they *working for* Diego?

CHAPTER **18**

"WE HAVE NO CHOICE," said Rita. "We have to check if the DEA is still in town."

"That could be dangerous," I replied, trying to sound profound. "You can't simply *spy* on the DEA while it's trying to spy on you."

We all looked at each other. It was one of those late nights in the garage. Kyra was all greasy from arguing with an engine's intake manifold and I was elbows-deep in a dead Buick. Rita had brought us clam chowder, which we drank from mugs. We three ladies do a terrible job of being dainty.

"We can't launch a war if they're sitting in the backseat waiting to yank the wheel," I said, as I took my arms out of the engine.

"Why not?" said Kyra.

"Because the next time we raid a convoy, they could put us in jail."

"No, *why not* as in why not spy on them?" clarified Kyra.

"What do you mean?" Rita set her mug down. It was one of those set your mug down types of proposals.

"We don't know if they're still here. I mean, if they're gone, if they're not even paying attention...then...then..."

"Then their entire visit was fake," concluded Rita. Which silenced us for a little bit.

Fake?

Later that night, Kyra and I ventured out to a few sketchy motels around town. Let the games begin.

We found one clerk idling in his office, watching shark attack videos on his laptop. The trick was to pretend we were the type of ladies who wanted to meet "dudes in suits." Which was doable because Kyra is blessed with the following problem: She looks like Audrey Hepburn. She looks so much like Audrey Hepburn, she spends most mornings dressing up to not look like her.

Except tonight.

Tonight she was doing recon. Civilian style. And she was wearing a cocktail dress and altitude shoes and talking like a bimbo. "Are there, are...y'know...eligible guys who might be...at the pool tomorrow...being eligible-y?" she said to the clerk.

This man was helpless before her. He said there was a ton of such guys. Smiled, pulled the toothpick from his mouth, and was delighted to try to pimp out his friends.

"No, no, no, more like, y'know...guys in suits...types," said Kyra. "Are there...that?"

"You wanna wrangle a fella in a suit?" The toothpick went back in the mouth.

"Does that type come in here?" I asked.

"Naw. Last June, we had some gents from the fishing expo. But they was bearded 'n' such. You like beards?" He stroked his beard.

"She doesn't." I pulled Kyra away.

Mission accomplished. No DEA there.

And the next two places would go exactly the same way. Some dude in flip-flops, feet up on the counter, telling us he hadn't seen a "suit" since last March, or since Reaganomics, or whatever.

Three hours later, we moved up a notch on the social spectrum and canvassed the hotels, too.

Obviously, this took a bit more ingenuity. You can't flirt with a desk manager who's young and busy and female and straight, who stands as merely one of three possible managers rotating shifts during any given week.

Nevertheless, we had to try.

"By any chance, have you seen either of these two gentlemen in here lately?"

We showed her, the desk manager, a photo on Kyra's phone of the billiard prince known as Warren Wright.

"Oh, I would've definitely recognized *him*," she said, ovaries on alert. "But, no, he wasn't here, sadly." She seemed to be telling the truth.

Five hotels and five conversations later, we were in the clear.

To go to war, of course.

CHAPTER 19

IMAGINE WALKING OUT TO your backyard in your otherwise normal, Plain Jane neighborhood, stopping by a wall just beyond the garage, moving a bush to the side, exposing a hatch in the dirt, looking around to make sure no one is watching you from down the street, or across the street, or anywhere at all, and opening the hatch to expose a dark, underground cavern.

Took us three shovels and a mini dozer, but we dug a tunnel.

Two days earlier, Rita had the idea that we needed a subterranean passageway. We got the inspiration from a busted mission she had led years ago. We were in Barranquilla, Colombia, chasing several bandits into a dark hut when, mere seconds later, the bandits vanished. They fled down a tunnel that crisscrossed their main boulevard underground, so that our teammates on the perimeter at street level could be evaded. It was annoyingly brilliant. Those bastards dug the passage with enough twists and turns at just the perfect angles to thoroughly shield their entire escape. Their layout created a very rough journey for anyone unfamiliar with the serpentine darkness. Yet for them, the *narcos,* it was like a second home.

We hated it. And loved it.

The day the DEA raided our garage and stole our most difficult-to-obtain weaponry, we became desperate for a plan B.

So now, we kept our stash eleven feet underground, buried along subterranean walls.

"Did you know Paris has underground tunnels?" said Kyra. "Full of bones and shit? I dated a Parisian once. He hated that I didn't smoke."

"This top area needs a buttress," said Rita. "This is where cars drive when our parking lot is full."

Rita was pointing to an area just beyond our heads. We had buttressed the tunnel entrance and the exit but this middle section was quite a task—to brace loose dirt to withstand the weight of six thousand pounds or more. That takes real engineering.

Kyra's brain could handle it. And did.

We even had a place to duck into in case both ends of the tunnel got breached. We built it at the vertex of the V-shape in the tunnel. This allowed us to fire on enemies from both directions, should we need to. This was worst-case scenario Armageddon-type thinking, but it's worth being overprepared.

So then the obvious question was, What's this tunnel really about?

This morning, we got the call we'd been waiting for. I was down the hole within minutes, heading for the far side. Rita and Kyra were both already there, gearing up. Strapping on Kevlar, lacing up boots. True, you need the very best gear when you're a three-person army. But today we were more than three, and we were in full kit.

We emerged from the tunnel into a copse of pecan trees about a quarter mile away from the café and the garage. We walked out onto a clearing two miles beyond the back hills. A secluded area. This would be a tough place for anyone in the vicinity to hear our noise.

Helicopter noise.

Three Bell Huey 600s sat whirling on the deep grass, awaiting us.

The best part about shiny packages was what's inside. Two of the pilots were from the Matamoros mission. Quiet and competent. They had a cargo of eighteen willing Marines. They'd heard of our exploits and wanted to help out. The Fat Man had arranged it, finally agreeing with my plea to really hit Diego where it hurt.

They saluted me. They saluted all three of us.

Kyra wiped tears from her eyes. She's all heart. Rita hides her emotions well, yet this stuff got to her, too. Me? I was mushy as custard inside. But I was a colonel again. And these troops needed me to be razor sharp.

This was the night Diego would never forget.

"Platoon," I shouted over the rotor noise, "let's make some history."

Oorah.

CHAPTER 20

AT AROUND 1:00 A.M. our choppers crossed into Mexico. The US border at certain points is fairly nondescript. You might not even realize that the two nations had swapped underneath you. But soon you start to see it. Even in the dark, you see it.

You ain't home no more.

The street lights are different. They're more randomly laid out. American towns tend to be a grid. Right angles and rows. Mexico is like a colony of lamps.

I was situated as a gunner. Seated at the handles of the .50 cal. For those who don't know, these bullets are massive, like mini-torpedoes that can rip through concrete at a rate of six hundred rounds per minute.

Normally the sniper takes the point, but I know this terrain better than anyone. And seeing as how this was an ill-advised, ill-conceived, illegal mission, it was crucial we didn't falter on any detail. Not one.

Tonight we were hunting something new.

Crops.

And I just spotted the first landmark on the way. Pitch black up ahead. "NV on," I called out to my gang via the radio headset. We flipped our night vision goggles on. Everything then became monochrome and anonymous. You have a range finder in the bottom of your view, telling you that that tree up ahead is seventy-nine meters away, telling you that the dope field on the right is seven hundred meters.

They're hard to spot from a distance, these crops, because the trees shield them from sight. But once your visual angle is correct, you can tell that up there on yonder hill lies a three-million-dollar crop of Diego Correra's finest herb.

And it would be a shame to just leave it by its lonesome.

CHAPTER 21

WE LET LOOSE ON six AGM Hellfire missiles. The dope field had no chance. The power of a Hellfire is unreal. Think of the impact of a monster truck barreling through a pillow fort in the middle of a freeway.

Overkill.

My favorite type of kill.

In the time it takes to spell the words *absolutely wrecked,* we absolutely wrecked about 150 acres of Diego's lifeblood. Lit it up like a backyard barbecue. Hillside gouged. Foliage fried.

"Platoon," I said into the radio. "Breakfast is cooked. Let's move on to lunch."

We coded our targets as follows:

"Breakfast" was the cluster of dope fields located thirty-five miles west of the Sierra Madre Occidental line, tucked just inside the Mexican border. Those fields were, *ahem,* gone now.

"Lunch" was a row of meth labs on the edge of a small town called La Resaca. This place was located twenty miles beyond the first fields. The trick was that it was nestled in between an elementary school and a pediatrics hospital. Not kidding. A school and a hospital. Thank you, Diego, for being the predictable douche we needed you to be.

"Dinner" was pure coca leaves. An entire crop of Colombian-grade cocaine located near the Gulf Coast. Diego's pride and joy. No other cartel on the continent had the technology to grow good coke this far north. Diego spent four million bucks to create the crops. His opus. And it would be last on our evening's raid menu.

But, en route to lunch, we encountered something we didn't think we'd face. "Contact left!" screamed Rita.

"Tangos on ridge, seven o'clock!" shouted the pilot.

A hailstorm of bullets whizzed past us. Lance Corporal Kagawa, a nice kid from Delaware, great sense of direction, terrible at karaoke, got his upper thigh ripped open by one of the random shots. "Ggggnnnnphhhhhh." He cringed.

I quickly slid over to his side of the helicopter. He was strapped in, there was no way he could fall out the open door, but a bullet hole is a bullet hole and I needed to stanch his bleeding ASAP.

"Man down," I called out into the radio.

We had a medic on our team, but the medic was in one of the other birds.

Yet that was about to be a very secondary concern. "RPG INCOMING!" my pilot yelled at the top of his lungs. You could hear what sounded like a jet engine whining in the distance, climbing the notes of a Doppler effect as it approached us at the terrifying pace of 650 miles per hour. An RPG hitting us would ignite our entire world in a huge midair explosion. Blades flying. Body parts soaring through the air. Flames singeing us at five thousand degrees. No thanks.

The first chopper dove left and downward. Smart pilot, Heather. She knew to fly into and askew from the oncoming RPG trajectory: A textbook move, but it's not easy to actually defy every survival instinct you have and turn *toward* an oncoming death projectile. The second chopper, my chopper, had to split in the other direction, which was obviously undesirable—

the maneuver meant exposing ourselves to a wider arc of vulnerability.

Luckily, or fatefully, the bandito who shot the first rocket at us severely underestimated that thing called gravity. Everyone does.

So he missed.

And the third chopper was well clear.

But the problem with in-air combat is that shooters who miss their first shot usually nail their second. Why? Because the RPG lights up the night sky with a lingering trail, so the shooter now knows exactly how to adjust his next trajectory.

Another problem was that an additional shooter might already be locked and loaded and waiting for us up ahead. Like the way you position two border collies to herd sheep into each other. There was a strong chance this potential second shooter would be up ahead in the ravine, prepared to take an easy shot at a slow-and-low bird.

Damn.

We were zipping down out of the sky, racing for airborne cover.

I took a kneeling stance, to aim out the door.

"Jack 'em up, Colonel," Kagawa rasped.

I readied my tiny little M16. A peashooter at a distance like this. The helicopter banked the opposite direction from my view, so, with our severe tilt upward, I had to pretty much aim down across our landing gear. I was scoped and ready to unleash a burst before I even knew where I was targeting.

"Gotta change speed," said the pilot.

I took a wild guess that Shooter number one would be higher than potential Shooter number two, so I aimed at a dark patch on the hillside.

Yup.

There he was, the clever chump. About to blast us to hell at pointblank. I let loose on three of the worst shots I'd ever shot. Hoping that my instincts about the same gravity that hurt his RPG would now *help* my return of fire.

Tap, tap, tap. Nailed him.

I'm lucky sometimes. Rarely. But sometimes.

"Nice shot, Coll," said the pilot.

But things were just getting started. Corporal Kagawa's upper leg was crooked and oozing blood. The second bird was alongside us. I could see the medic looking over at me and my wounded friend from his perch in his bird's doorway. The good news was that we had a chance to stabilize him on our own. The bad news was that there were more RPG shooters up ahead and a small plane on the horizon.

If we were going to dust the next target, we were going to have to do it on the run.

"Condor Two to Condor Five, advise descent to one-five meters," said my pilot. He was calling out the new altitude to fly at. Fifteen meters. Fifteen teeny little meters. We were descending below the tree line so that visual detection was as hard as possible for our enemies.

Up ahead were the lights on the children's hospital, which were shining across from the soccer field for the elementary school. Sandwiched in between, in the dark buildings, was the meth lab. I was mounted with my trusty M16. Kyra was now on the .50 cal. Rita was coming over to me to try and stop the blood gushing out of Kagawa's leg.

"Small plane, fifteen miles north by northeast," said my pilot. "Approaching fast."

Kyra was now on point surveying the upcoming groundwork, laying out her assessment of our tactical options for me: "We can either scrap target two and race these guys to three, or we get as low as possible to hit the labs. Your call, Colonel."

It was indeed my tough decision. We were facing a small Beechcraft Bonanza plane on the horizon, which didn't have missiles but certainly had the ability to blitz our choppers from above by dropping random items onto our blades.

Would that work?

Very possibly, yes. Helicopters don't like to have their dainty little private parts touched. Not by you, not by me, not by their boyfriends, no one. They will literally rip themselves apart in self-hate if the rear rotor gets out of sync with the main rotor. The torque is maniacal. The birds go down. Hard. Ugly.

So, yes, that plane rapidly approaching us on the horizon— that little bugger was the potential kiss of death.

But it wasn't here yet.

I got on the radio to tell the platoon my decision, to tell them exactly what they were praying to hear.

"Time for lunch."

CHAPTER 22

THE TRICK WITH A quick bombing run is to be as comprehensive as possible during the one pass you make. Instead of doing multiple passes, you want to do one, just one. And it needs to count.

Ironically, to speed things up, you need to slow things down.

We were originally planning for fifty-mile-per-hour attack patterns. Straight routes. Repeated three times.

Now, instead, we were going to fly zigzag. One pass. "Slow," I said to the pilot. "Slowwwww. Slower than a bureaucrat." I wanted this win badly. I couldn't risk a clumsy attack.

Over the next crest, we'd find the small orchard we'd use as a landmark. Then beyond that would be the outskirts of La Resaca.

"I'm really s-sorry," mumbled Corporal Kagawa. He was writhing in pain but also trying to prevent his lower half from squirming too much. He didn't want to draw attention to himself.

"You're good, bro," I said, readjusting his compress. "Just imagine how much ass you're gonna get thanks to this."

"I'm . . . picturing that one chick in the 304th," he replied. "Asking her to marry me an' shit." And then, after some more writhing and moaning, "Sorry I messed up."

There's nothing worse than feeling like you let your teammates down. I knew his pain all too well. And it got me losing focus a bit. It's the bone-crushing guilt trip that I'd already been cultivating inside my soul, watering it, fertilizing it, nurturing it into a huge treelike thing. A guilt forest, actually. The knowledge that I'd led my crew on mission after mission and we had yet to stop Diego. That I got my buddies into danger. That I lost my entire family. That Corporal Kagawa now had a splintered upper thigh and was bleeding pretty bad.

"Does he need immediate aid?" I asked Rita.

He wouldn't let her reply. "Don't you dare turn us back, Colonel."

"He can hold out," said Rita, "but he's leaky."

She was right—the gauze she kept refreshing for the wound was getting soaked disturbingly quickly.

"Don't," said Kagawa. "Don't, Colonel. Please?"

I know that face. I know that plea. It would positively destroy this youngster if I turned us around because of his injury.

I grabbed his hand. An assurance. From here on out, this was for him. This was for faith in the team. *Got your back, little brother.* "Okay," I said to him. "But I order you to cease bleeding."

He laughed at my cheesy line. It was the first time his face stopped wincing.

"Banking hard right," said the pilot. We were about to emerge into plain view of the target. And we were about to be in range of their turret. Yes, they had a turret.

"Technical. Far corner," said Kyra, spotting enemy armament. When a bandito mounts a big-ass gun to the back of his dinky-ass Toyota, that's called a technical. One might think this is slumming it and that it's trivial, but banditos live and die by this crap. Little pickup trucks with nasty-ass weapons on back. They're mobile and they shoot hard.

"Platoon," I said into the radio. "Friendly reminder: We don't touch the school, we don't touch the hospital. Target is the dark row of buildings in the middle."

Our two birds diverged into the woods. Just above the treetops. The obvious move was to torch the fields from the far side, but our goal was to do the exact opposite of what was expected.

"Cleared hot," I told my pilots, meaning anyone at any time could open fire.

Condor Five banked over the outer edge of the crop. My bird, Condor Two, was coming up on the rear of the hut.

"Castle in range," said the pilot "*Eyes on* at 150 meters and closing."

"Tech! Small road!" shouted Kyra, immediately firing at a technical speeding along our right side. The dude in the back was on a mounted PK machine gun. Pointed at us.

He didn't stink at aiming. He managed to spray a good amount of bullets right at our belly, and, since we didn't know how close he was, his salvo caught us off guard.

But Kyra is no slouch in bed. With a second barrage, she massacred the front of the Toyota and, yes, flipped it on its side, throwing the guy in back deep into the bush.

Now our co-pilot was going to work on the meth lab. "Target acquired. Firing away."

Both pilots then clicked that little red switch just under the right thumb, the one that first needs a clearance toggled from the main console, the one that was cleared half a minute ago, the one that sends about eight hundred pounds of fireworks forward from the bottom of the chopper, and, holy shit, pulverizes a goddamn meth lab.

Every crevice of that compound went up in flames at once. A white volcano. Bright as hell. Loud as God.

It's like I got to kick Diego in his favorite nut.

CHAPTER 23

THE METH LAB AT location two was a roaring inferno. We had served breakfast and lunch. We had finished the easy part.

Word would have already gotten to the ranch hands at location three, dinner, by the time we were en route, a thirty-five-minute journey. Enemy trucks were already on the way to intercept us along with that small plane creeping up on our rear.

Corporal Kagawa was bleeding like crazy, which meant his body defied my official orders to coagulate, but he found enough strength to clamp down on his wound on his own. Rita didn't want to let him be the one to do it, but I told her she had to.

Why?

Because the kid needed to feel like he had something to do. Even if he was doing a worse job than she would. His body needed the feeling of responsibility so that his immune system could fight harder inside him. The potential stress of him knowing he was depriving Rita of her combat assignment would've probably eaten him alive.

"Two klicks and closing," said our pilot. "Firing on your mark."

"Copy that, Condor Two. On your flank. Evasive will be down and left."

"Down and left, affirmative. Will mirror."

The two pilots were agreeing on what path of rapid evasive maneuver they would each take in the event they were both surprised and had to scurry. Two helicopters accidentally touching in any way is about as desirable as getting dental work done in the middle of a rodeo. A helicopter is the most delicate contraption ever invented, and it operates amid a hurricane of force—let's just say it's super damn jealous of other helicopters.

"Firing away." Once again the pilots unleashed the Hellfire missiles, and the world in front of me exploded. We had crushed the entire crop into a massive cloud of heat and fury. We had won.

That was my thought for about a fraction of a second. Then came a rather strange problem.

"Horses," said Kyra.

"What?" I said.

"Horses, ten o'clock," Rita was pointing to the center of what was a large, quickly shrinking doughnut of fire.

I looked down and saw it. We were set to bank hard back toward the hillside and get the hell home, we were officially done—but there were three horses in the middle of the burning field.

Protocol says you can't risk soldiers to save animals. But my crew was rabidly fond of horses.

"Can't leave 'em, Coll," said Kagawa.

"No way," agreed a couple of other troops, including Rita.

There was a path through the circle of confusion that would allow the mare and her foals to head directly out of the fire. But the three animals were absolutely terrified and unable to recognize salvation. To be honest, if I were down there at ground level, I doubt I'd see it either. Those poor things would have to gallop across a football-field's worth of flaming cocaine before they could be safe.

Why in God's name someone tied three horses in the middle

of a coke field I'll never know, but the reason really didn't matter. The hope was that they weren't tethered.

"Contact hillside!" said the pilot. And of course we were now getting peppered by AK-47s, a group of banditos shooting from the edge of the forest hill.

Our bird, Condor Two, was about to rip them to shreds, but Condor Five was hovering too close to our line of attack. One of the horses was trotting tragically toward the heart of the fire and the troops aboard Five were trying to deter it. Just as bullets were coming at us from more AK-47s. This shit was insane. We had never been this scattered.

I blamed myself for pushing dinner without proper recon.

Rookie mistake.

The Condor Five pilot leveled his bird out, giving us a trajectory, and my second gunner and second assistant team leader unleashed about seven hundred rounds of ammo toward the far side of the field.

We had herded the horses a bit. The first two made it across the path. The third one was on fire, literally on fire, thanks to the cloth blanket on his saddle, and was about to leap over the gap, too. We were so inexplicably excited about this. All of us. Going nuts. Like watching a running back break loose on a game-winning touchdown.

"Go, homeboy!" shouted Kyra. "Go!"

He was about to cross. He was about two strides from completion. And the banditos shot him.

Shot him dead.

An intentional barrage hit his head and torso as the animal buckled and tumbled into an ugly heap, sliding across the dirt. We freaked out. All of us. He still had some zest in him. He knew where his safety zone was now. And he was trying to drag the back half of his magnificent body toward the promised land.

But his limbs couldn't do it. His front hooves were clawing the dirt. He was pulling hard. There was no quit in that little muchacho. But the physics were against him. Christ. If there ever there was a way to piss on your enemy's morale in the midst of battle, this was it. There was zero tactical reason to shoot the animal. Zero.

"Permission to vacate," the pilot said to me.

Not sure what would be waiting for me back home in Texas: what kind of self-inflicted mood would be lurking in my subconscious. Would I be happy? Relieved? Proud? Stuck on a horse? We had consumed all three meals but as I looked across to the faces in the other two helicopters, looking past the sullen faces in our own cabin, I could tell that this entire platoon was fixated on the animal.

"Mission over," I replied. "Take us anywhere but here."

And we headed out.

It's hard to savor a vague victory. Did we win? Did they win? If they would shoot down their own horse just to spite us, how much damage did we really do to them? How much closer was I to Diego's capture?

To answer my original question, yes there was something waiting for me back in Archer, Texas, that's for sure. I found out as soon as I settled inside my house.

I was about to be kidnapped.

CHAPTER 24

THE TASTE OF VICTORY was short lived. Whatever ground we just gained only sought to remind me that we hadn't gotten him yet.

When I come home after a mission, I like to take a hot shower. Sounds trivial but there's something about the steam and the acoustics. You can sing anything in there and you feel like a rock diva. Plus you get cleaner. Plus your muscles relax. Plus it's a way of procrastinating whatever long-ass litany of crap you have on your to-do list, like item thirty-seven: Kill stupid Diego Correra. Still.

I had been under the shower nozzle for about half my usual epic stay, shampooing and just beginning a full-body soap down, when I heard the first squeak.

I turned off the water and stood there. Listening. Did I seriously just hear something in my house? A noise?

Unlike the cute visit to the garage by the DEA, this whatever-it-was noise wasn't quiet. It sounded as if someone's shoulder bumped into a wall, the wooden beam behind the plaster contorting under instant pressure.

I stood there, naked, not breathing, my hand still on the shower knob.

I instantly realized it was better for me to keep moving

around—silent inaction would alert anyone in the house, any intruders, that I knew something was up. I wanted them to think I knew nothing.

I stepped out of the shower. I had two towels ready to go, folded neatly on the sink counter. Way over there. By the time I had taken two steps toward the towels, I heard a door shut.

My heart started racing. *Shit.* This wasn't my imagination. This was an actual intrusion.

I needed a weapon in my hand. Across the hall I had a Walther PPK stashed. Yes, that's the James Bond gun. Yes, it's small. And amazing. If I could just turn off the bathroom lights and dart across the hall and arm myself, I could make a mad dash for the guest bedroom and get out through the window, assuming they had both doors guarded.

But before I could even start to consider how long this would all take, the bathroom knob started turning. On its own. Slowly.

It took about three seconds max, but it felt like super slow motion every step of the way. The knob turned, and I lunged forward, went low to duck under any line of fire, to intercept the opponent rather than retreat deeper into the bathroom where I would be weaponless and easy to shoot. I'd love to claim that I grabbed some perfume and a BIC lighter and made a blowtorch or that I ripped the shower curtain rod from the stall and wielded a Martha Stewart spear, but I'm not that clever. Besides, I don't wear perfume. And is that crap really flammable? My bathroom, as I noted in that millisecond of combat prep, was sadly lacking in sharp objects. I had a bar of fragrant soap. That was it. From a crouched position, still midstride, I let the door open just enough so I could access my enemy's weapon. Utilizing Krav Maga techniques, I could snatch it.

The first thing I saw through that door was, yes, a gun. But that's when the lights went out.

And so I was in the dark, weaponless, grabbing at a Glock from the grip of what I came to discover was a 240-pound ogre, while I stood with wet feet on a slippery floor.

Naked.

I punched at his ribs. The ogre. I wanted to grab a handful of torso skin and just twist the hell out of it, twist and pull downward, but he had on a big poofy jacket. We grappled for a long, silent, respectable four seconds. But he was on a mission. And his mission was completed rather quickly. Before I could strike even one blow, my neck was jabbed with a needle by another assailant. His partner. And, within seconds, precious seconds, my ability to struggle expired. And my hands and legs were cuffed. And a hood came over my head. And the darkness got even darker.

CHAPTER 25

ANYONE WHO'S HAD THE flu has had those weird-as-hell vivid dreams. You get this whacked-out mixture of reality and surreality. You come in and out of being awake. Sweating. Feverish. Unsure whether anything that just happened in your mind happened for real. This, my friends, is exactly what it's like to be drugged and hooded.

Hood on, obviously I couldn't see much. The first sensation I had was hearing something. It was murmuring coming from the far corner of the room. Two males. Middle-aged. Whispering. Stopping every minute or so, as if to glance over at me. I heard snatches of their strange conversation: "...or before the other one checks in..." and then "...sure if the other doesn't..."

I couldn't tell where these guys were from. To tell the truth, I didn't even recognize the accent, or whether they even *had* accents.

Suddenly, I was approached by a guy whose knuckles smelled like kerosene.

Offering me a drink of water, he removed my gag and lifted my hood—just enough for me to look down across my cheekbones and across the room. I tried to take a mental photograph so I could study it in my head after I glimpsed it:

1. On the far side of the room were two guys in track jackets. They had guns. An M24 and an M5.
2. The room was big and bare. Not much furniture.
3. There was a doorway, and through it I caught a glimpse of a tire. The tire of some kind of vehicle.
4. The tire was mounted on an airplane wheel.

It took me a split second but I quickly realized that I was in a hangar.

The hood was yanked back down over my face, and Kerosene Hands stuffed the gag back in my mouth. I heard some whispering behind me. And then I heard a yelp from what sounded like another room. A female voice. Muffled. Crying out. I didn't know for sure it was Kyra, but I certainly suspected it. Then I heard some more whispering and a large metal object clanging against something.

Goddammit, you dogs. Don't hurt her.

That's what I tried to say. Those six words. But I was gagged.

I assumed six hours had passed since they put the gag on me.

But I have no idea if it was six or three. Or sixteen. Or sixty. The hood ensured that I couldn't see any daylight. You can learn a lot from daylight. The height of the sun in the sky. The apex of its arc. The fact that it's out, at all. The difference in angle fifteen minutes between glances, if you're lucky enough to get a second glance, can tell you where north is.

Every little bit of info counts.

I wasn't going to get that far, though. I could already hear what sounded like a hierarchy of conversation. Somewhere off to my left I detected what was distinctly a verbal command: not two guys talking but one guy telling another guy what the hell to do.

There's my fulcrum.

I made up my mind that the next time they came to give me

water or raise my hood or take a look at my sulky disposition I was going to spit out the gag and bite the hand that reached in. I was going to bite the damn thing as hard as possible and see if that little oral *hello* could get them to change their plan.

Because I was now convinced Kyra was tied up in the next room and was being ordered onto that plane.

And if that plane was going to Mexico, death would be a luxury.

CHAPTER 26

THERE REALLY IS NO way to escape a situation like this. Not if it unfolds as planned. The plan, their plan, was that I'd be cuffed to my chair. Hooded. There were armed men in the room. They knew where I was. I didn't. They knew what they intended to do with me. I didn't. They knew who they were. I had no clue.

That meant I'd be worse than dead if I let their plan unfold.

I had to derail it somehow.

Even if it was just a tiny hiccup in their agenda. I had to prod the tissue of their intentions with a surgical instrument: to see how it responds, gain an edge. Because if I bite the ideal guy's hand, he will want to beat the living shit out of me. And if he's not *allowed* to do that yet, then I might cause a conflict between him and whoever *is* in charge.

But that's not how this day would go.

"I don't care, just get it done," said the voice in charge.

My hood got lifted off. And before I could bite the guy who was lifting it off, I saw his face. And you know whose face it was?

Warren Wright. I should call him El Warren. Warren Wrong. I don't know how he slipped his allegiance from the DEA to Diego Correra, but he must have. The shit-sucking brickhead.

"Colonel," he said. "I need you to keep your mouth shut. Just do as you're told and you won't get hurt."

I wanted to say the following: "Pretty much whatever you tell me to do, I'm going to do the opposite." But I was gagged, so it sounded like "Heehee muh heheheh hoo." And I gave up halfway through.

"Stop moving," said Warren.

If I could just get him in a choke hold, maybe get my hand around his voice box and threaten to yank it out, I could get his minions to let me bargain for Kyra's life.

But my handcuffs were tight. Too tight.

"Stop moving!" barked Warren.

I moved even harder.

"STOP!" he shouted, then added, "Trust me."

I stopped.

Not because he told me to stop and certainly not because he told me to trust him. *Trust you, you little bitch? I'd rather trust a garbage fire.* But because I heard something in the background that was an absolute game changer.

The plane was starting its engines.

CHAPTER 27

I MUST HAVE LOST consciousness again, because the next thing I knew I was on that plane, with a pounding headache. They put silencing-headphones over my ears so I couldn't hear anything. Hooded, gagged, and cuffed, I could barely tell if I was sitting or standing. The only sensation I felt were changes in altitude, which, let's face it, with all my other senses deprived, made me wanna puke up everything I had eaten in the past year.

At this point I was barely maintaining the combat initiative. They won, whoever they were. They owned the day. I was being taken to where they intended me to be taken. The only thing I had control of was my thoughts. And I couldn't even control those. Certain unwanted images kept floating relentlessly to mind. Namely, my youngest daughter.

"Trust yourself," she said.

Myself? How? Why?

The word *trust* was popping up because Warren had said it. I reminded myself that my sensory-deprived brain was just misfiring its synapses, bringing random memories to the forefront, blending new memories with old ones.

I'd failed, as a soldier. I managed to get my ass abducted. All because I simply *had* to take an ill-advised shower. I didn't have the good sense to check my house before getting naked and vulnerable, before separating myself from my weapon. A cardinal sin. And I had committed it.

"Mommy, you can do this," said my implausible daughter.

Do what? Was I hallucinating? She hadn't aged—my vision of her. It had been two years, but she wasn't any taller. Sensory deprivation is guaranteed to fry you into mental anguish. No one survives it.

"Stay awake, Mommy."

"I am awake, munchkin. I'm just sort of losing the battle right now. Don't look at Mommy. Look at the sunrise over—"

Wham! Somebody hit me with a baseball bat. Aluminum. Hard as a slugger.

Here in this plane.

No, not a bat. It was a rib of the aircraft cargo area. I was lying down. This was the metal support, the curved girder that braces the fuselage.

I felt a pair of large hands move me back to whatever position I was in. I think we hit turbulence. Nobody hit me, actually. It was the air. The air hit us all.

Or, no, wait a minute.

We were landing.

CHAPTER 28

I WAS IN THE middle of a warehouse. In a chair. Cuffed. Muffed. Hooded. When the blinders finally came off, I had to squint. My vision was blurry. Everything was so bright. I couldn't tell if it was the next day or the next week. There were two guards posted at the main door to the warehouse. I could hear some footsteps echoing in the distance. They were coming from behind. My captors. The boss of my captors. I didn't even turn. My final middle finger. Let them look at the back of my uninterested head.

I want to say I could smell his aftershave or his stench, but I couldn't. I could only just hear him. Warren.

Warren Never Wright.

"I'll need your full attention, Colonel," he said.

The thing is, based on yet another weird exchange of murmurs I caught just now, I realized it wasn't Warren who was in charge of this abduction. I heard a pair of high-heeled feet approaching. I'd recognize those shoes anywhere. Patent black leather asexual heels. Retail cost $69.99 at the naval base store. We ladies all had to buy a pair. And she was wearing hers.

General Claire Dolan.

She stood in front of me in full uniform. She had enough brass on her chest to outshine a pride parade.

"Sorry about the methodology, Colonel," she said to me in her standard bludgeoning tone. One doesn't get to the rank of general without tapping into one's inner mega-bitch. But she might not necessarily be here to ruin my life. "I hope you're physically undamaged."

I didn't say yes.

"I hope you're mentally undamaged," she added.

I'd worked under her Fifth Battalion six years ago. She was tyrannical, ruthless, and played her favorites, but she absolutely positively always got her job done. Something that's been hard for me to relate to lately.

"I'm here to ask you about your informant," she said. "Where are you getting your information from . . . about Diego Correra?"

I wasn't going to answer anything until she assured me that Kyra and Rita were all right. If she was worth even one stripe on her rainbow scoop of medals, she'd quickly tell me that my two spiritual sisters were fine.

"Who is your leak?"

I didn't answer.

She pulled up a chair really close to me and sat down. She took out a ballpoint pen from her coat pocket. I started to get the feeling that they'd ask me this question over and over until I gave in.

She started to whisper really close to my ear. "I know you've done a lot for your country. I know what happened after Matamoros. I know the price you've paid. Prices." She leaned in even closer, talked even quieter. "You have my condolences. You have my sympathies. You have my prayers to the God of your choosing. But you *don't* have my patience. *Who. Is. Your. Leak?*"

If I knew, I still wouldn't tell you.

I sat unmoved. She took a deep breath in. She hovered her pen near the canal of my ear. Not in it. But around it. Hovering. She could poke my eardrum. Tidy. It would be easy for her to deny it afterward, easy to say it got punctured on its own. Perforated. It would be easy for her to deny touching me. Perforated eardrums hurt like crazy.

"You rose through the ranks pretty damn quick," she said, launching one of those *here is your dossier, you soon-to-be-dead tramp* monologues. "Almost as quick as my royal ass. You paid your dues. Got the desk job promotion with the privilege of staying in the field. You did what any good rookie does, you made male officers jealous. Now, I don't want to have to ask this one more time . . ."

"Who is your leak?" yelled Wright.

His voice echoed in this warehouse. If General Dolan seemed annoyed, Agent Wright seemed downright enraged. Not sure how I could be the source of his intense exasperation, given that I'm the one who sat under a hood for a day. Maybe he just hated that he was being dragged alongside me. Locked in this trash dump of a warehouse, wherever the hell this was.

"I'm not gonna keep waiting for an answer," said Warren.

Luckily for us all, Dolan finally said the magic words. "Sergeant Holmes and Lieutenant Ramirez are fine."

So I spoke up.

"I want verification," I said to her. "I want to be treated like a human being."

"Then act like a colonel."

"I'm not a colonel anymore," which was a fine thing to say, but then I stumbled right into what was clearly her verbal trap. "I was discharged two years ago."

"Yet you prance around . . . all around the continent . . . shooting villagers and setting shit on fire."

"Villagers?" I had to correct her. *"Murderers!"*

"You don't raise your voice at us!" said Warren, who at this point was fuming, who stood up and kicked his metal folding chair across the room. "Not us!"

I'm guessing he'd promised Dolan I'd cooperate instantly. It started to seem more and more likely to me that they had already questioned me while I was drugged and that maybe I didn't say jack to them. Even while drugged. High five to Drugged Amanda and Her Stubborn-as-a-Morgue Mouth.

Warren kept yelling and was clearly ready to take over the whole interrogation. "You put the lives of hundreds of agents in jeopardy."

Yes, sir, I did.

"Compromised US–Mexico diplomatic relations."

Yes, sir, I did.

"Committed enough criminal acts to be tied up in a box for life."

"You have no proof of any of that," I said to him. Loud. Turning to give him the direct eye contact he probably didn't want. Bully. "If you did, we wouldn't be talking in a warehouse."

He leaned in. "You better hope there isn't some sort of Geneva Convention thing you're relying on in your head right now, thinking, *hoping,* that we don't get out some power tools and Guantánamo you into a more cooperative bitch."

"If Rita and Kyra are in the next room, then prove it to me," I said.

He stood there. Unflinching.

"If all you want is the name of a leak," I continued, "I don't *have* the name of a leak. This conversation is over, so take us home."

"No," said Dolan.

"Well, then we'll just stay here for a really long time and trade beauty tips," I said. I'd lost my cool at this point. "Who does your beehive? When was the last time you rechiseled it? Was it here? In this room? And by any chance are you gonna tell me where the hell this shit hole is?"

General Dolan stood up, a sneer forming on her face. "You're in Mexico City, babe. You wanna leave?" She tossed the pen in my lap and added, "Find your own way home."

CHAPTER 29

"FIND YOUR OWN way home?" questioned Rita. "That's what she said to you?"

"Let's not worry about it," I replied.

"I hate that whore," said Kyra. "Always have."

The three of us were literally standing on a street corner in what felt like, by American standards, a back alley, but what was really, by Mexico City standards, an actual street. Quaint, with little colorful stores and square houses all sandwiched together. The whole thing would be lovely if it weren't so run down. This was the bad part of town in Mexico City, Distrito Federal.

"That's north," said Rita, pointing eighty degrees to the right of the setting sun.

"Find your own way home," repeated Kyra. "How about my boot finds its way up your ass?"

"That would be fun but you're not wearing boots," said Rita.

None of us were. They had left us in almost nothing worth wearing outdoors. We barely had the clothes on our backs. All jokes and wardrobe malfunctions aside, we had a more horrific problem looming over us now. We had literally nothing. No weapons. No car. No bikes. No phones. No cash. No credit cards. No food. No water. I had on a pair of prison-issue overalls and sandals, which was only *slightly* better than the towel I was wearing when they brought me in. Kyra was in yoga pants and a T-shirt. Rita was rocking mom jeans and a turtleneck sweater.

"We can't stay in one place," I said, adopting command mode. "We have to keep walking."

"Yes, ma'am," said both of my best friends, snapping into soldier mode.

I pointed across the street and we crossed. We began our hike. "Are either of you hurt?"

"My everlasting love for the Marine Corps is hurt," said Kyra. "But, no, other than that, my body is a flawless temple and that temple is ready to do some really un-Zen things."

"I'm fine," said Rita, "physically and mentally. They didn't torture us. Are we really gonna walk to Texas?"

She was only 38 percent kidding.

I didn't answer her. I honestly had no idea how we were going to get back. This situation would be hard enough for normal people to undo, but for the three of us, who were high-profile targets for every kind of bad intention from every kind of a bad-intending person, we were in for a long night.

Dolan didn't get promoted to general based on her sagging tits. She was a ruthless witch, who out-ass-kicked in every ass-kicking contest she entered. And she entered all of them. If she felt a mission needed to be done a certain way, she would destroy whoever contradicted her. And she would get that mission done. Had to tip my hat to that. But she hated me. Not sure why. I had never spoken to her face-to-face before today, but I'd hear things around the base. She wanted me erased from the Corps.

She couldn't kill me. But technically she could certainly find a situation to let me die in. Here. In Mexico.

And would Warren Wright stop her? Apparently not.

"Do you think we'll see any hostiles?" asked Rita.

"Affirmative," I replied.

"What exactly should we be on the lookout for?" she asked.

"Them," I said, pointing across the street.

There were four guys standing at the far end of the block. Locals. Mean-looking.

It would be better if they just wanted to *do* us. We could repel that sort of thing. But they didn't have that sort of "do" in mind.

CHAPTER 30

"THEY COULD BE DRUNK," said Kyra.

At this point we had walked several blocks in a tangential path that took us away from whatever barrio our four enemies spawned from. We would stop to point at shit in store windows so that we could yap with each other like giggly little tourists, so that we could happen to glance to our rear without looking like we were glancing to our rear.

This is how we could monitor them. This is how we confirmed that, damn it, they were still there.

"They're following us way too well to be drunk," replied Rita.

Indeed, they were. We picked up the pace. We fast-walked down the tiny streets, turning abruptly, turning again, crossing, crossing back. Not exactly in a full-fledged sprint to evade them, no. We didn't want to take it to the next level just yet, not without further information, like whether they were armed, what they were armed with, whether they had friends up ahead of us. We didn't even know if they were using cell phones.

Every time we turned, we'd lose them for about a half block, and then we'd see them come around the corner right behind us. Still on track. It was eerie.

"They might have eyes above," said Kyra.

Yes.

Overwatch. A situation with one of those old ladies, a native, pretending to reel in her laundry line, *squeakity-squeak,* while actually scouting the three of us from her third-floor window. The majority of the neighborhood was two stories, so anyone with any kind of additional height could see us gringas from a mile away.

"Turn here," I said, as we then ducked behind a tight alley. "Definitely caught sight of a handgun on the pudgy one. I'm guessing the others have knives."

The fastest-moving of the four guys was a youngish looking chap, maybe twenty years old. He looked agile. Probably good at parkour. Probably just dying to impress his buddies and get extra violent with me and my lady friends.

"Do you think they're connected to Diego?" asked Rita.

I quickly peeked my eye around the edge of the wall and took a brief look at each one.

"Worse," I replied. I was starting to realize we were in for a rough trip. "I think they're cops."

I needed to take us into the smallest possible area. The problem with cops is they'd have a very close network of radio communication. Probably the best in town. I was already dismayed by the presence of four dudes tailing us—but then there was the prospect of another, let's say, *ten* joining in...

"I dunno that we can ditch 'em," said Rita, "here in their own backyard."

"This place is like a maze," agreed Kyra.

"We're not trying to ditch 'em," I replied.

I repositioned the ballpoint pen in my clenched fist. The one General Dolan dropped in my lap. The one I now had gripped like a dagger.

"We're about to start the party," I said.

CHAPTER 31

WE ROUNDED THE CORNER into a narrow alley, wide enough for maybe one horse or one cow or moose or whatever-the-hell transport animal this stupid ghetto was founded on. It was narrow as shit. One horse on a diet. There were stoops and inset doorways. Those were perfect for us. We readied ourselves in three separate positions. Rita and I tucked ourselves into two different doorways while Kyra kept walking toward the deep dead end in plain sight.

Visual bait.

I could hear some commotion just around the corner. The four men were approaching. We had no weapons except my pen, but we had the element of surprise. What we wanted was the first guy to be well ahead of his pack. He would then round the corner alone, and we could ambush him and take his gun or knife. Then do the same thing to the next person.

I was calming my breath. Listening. Staying loose. I was planning to deliver a swift pen stab to the clavicle.

But that clavicle never arrived.

Whatever lone-vulnerable-pursuer-Disney-perfection-scenario I'd envisioned did not come to fruition at all. Kyra was correct. These guys knew their backstreets like the back of their hand. Instead of us trapping one of the four guys in these tight quarters, those four guys had trapped us in a small city alley.

I could hear the pudgy one yell to his buddy down the block. Something about "staking" it. They were positioning themselves at the four sides.

Kyra finally checked back over her shoulder to see how we were doing. She saw the cancel signal from Rita and quickly returned to us. No talking, no making sounds—we signed each other the following:

Four enemies. Surrounding. We run. That way. One mile.

That was it.

That was our entire plan. We were going to improvise the hell out of this. Because I had no idea if those four guys were packing machetes or if they all had firepower. We braced ourselves. And then I nodded.

Let's do this.

We all three ran through the back door of a small taqueria in a dead sprint and emerged onto another street. It became instantly clear that I was wrong about there being only four guys.

Now there were twenty-four.

And they had submachine guns. And they were using them.

CHAPTER 32

WE RAN AS LOW as we could with as much zigzag as efficiency would allow. We were dodging every kind of third-world-Kalashnikov bullet they had in stock, from seemingly every direction.

We ran hard, directly into the first open door we could find, a laundromat, with zero time to assess anything at all, just banking on the possibility there might be a back door and that, through it, there might be another tiny alley like the previous one.

There was.

We ran down the alley, and I skidded to a stop along the gravel to try to open the first back door that looked accessible. It wasn't, and neither was the second, but the third—the door to a dive bar—was, and I burst it open just as Kyra and Rita ran in behind by me, just as a wash of thirty more bullets embedded themselves in the wall where my head had been merely two seconds prior.

We were back out on the streets.

At this point there was no way to survive by continuing to flee. Soon, very soon, statistics would catch up with us and the law of mathematical probability would dictate that a random round from a random gun fired by a randomly aiming shooter was going to find its way into one of our torsos. That is, *if* we kept exposing our torsos to submachine-gun fire while running in a straight line away from young men who have memorized every straight line in the neighborhood.

I was desperate to recreate the setting for the failed ambush we tried earlier but I was too scared to sacrifice our current velocity. After about five minutes, I think we'd seriously traveled one entire mile. You'd be shocked to learn just how damn fast you can run when guns are behind you. We had emerged out of the heart of one of the most dangerous neighborhoods in the world: Iztapalapa, a barrio of Distrito Federal. Poor, run-down. A virtual playground for criminals.

"If we can cross into the center of the city," shouted Rita as we sprinted, "I seriously doubt they'll follow us."

"No, no, no," yelled Kyra. "They'll go anywhere. They're not allowed to lose us. That's their pride."

"So we have to square up with them," I yelled back.

"With all twenty? All twenty of these guys?" shouted Rita.

"No," I replied. "The first four. The cops."

We were running down a gradual hill. To our right was the legendary Cerro de la Estrella, a national park with a small, remarkable mountain of history. Actually everything around here is charming to look at if you simply subtract the poverty, misogyny, oppression, depression, pollution, corruption, and daily violence.

None of the locals would help us. Doors were closing ahead of us. We could see curtains being drawn. Cars turning away from our direction. Pedestrians ducking into shops.

As soon as anyone saw us, fear governed their next move.

I don't know how fast word can spread in a city of sixteen million people, but this neighborhood had its own little ecosystem. Its own self-sustaining misery. *Welcome to Iztapalapa: Three Days Since Our Last Lynching.*

"The last corner on the left," I shouted to Rita and Kyra.

Still sprinting, we rounded yet another corner. I think we had logged three miles in fifteen minutes. We were close to Avenue Río Churubusco, which meant we were on the way to downtown. To "civilization." Close to exiting the Iztapalapan war zone.

But instead of finding an area to trap our captors, we found ourselves trapping ourselves. Again. In a dead-end corridor. With no alcoves or inset doorways for cover. Not even a cardboard box.

Ladies and gentlemen, the world's cleanest damn back alley.

And I managed to find it. And I managed to lead Rita into it and somehow managed to lose Kyra at the same time. We weren't together! Jesus.

And then, finally, as if on cue, at the worst time possible, those first four bastards showed up. Guns ready. They were looking to shoot the living shit out of us. In tight quarters.

Perfect.

CHAPTER 33

"HANDS UP!" YELLED Officer Whatever-The-Hell-His-Name-Was.

"*¡Los manos, puta!*" said his sidekick. "*¡Levante los manos!*"

Rita and I were cornered.

There was obviously a huge reward paid to whoever captured us, but something sinister, something ulterior, could be seen growing in the eyes of officer number three. Let's call him Señor Sleazy, muscling his way to the front row. He had some stripes on his sleeve, so I guessed he was the local captain and the three guys around him were his sergeants and fluffers.

"On your knees," said Captain Sleazy.

Rita and I traded a look. We knew what this one meant.

"On your knees, *puta,*" he said again.

The guy behind him, let's call him Officer Double Chin for obvious reasons, started murmuring some inaudible crap into his radio. They were telling the rest of their gang to do whatever. I didn't like the sound of it—directions to hang back. I hadn't seen Kyra since two blocks ago. If these slimy reptiles had their hands on her, a pretty girl like her, I can't even imagine what they'd already be doing.

"*Estamos solo turistas,*" I protested. *We're just tourists.* "*Queremos visitar,* er, the museum."

Wham, I felt a kick into the back of my knee, which sent me down onto the pavement in a forced kneel. Double Chin didn't like my Spanish conjugation.

Rita immediately knelt alongside me. Cooperating. She knew that defiance was my prerogative, not hers. She knew to follow my lead. We were down, execution style. Would they do it right there? I was the political prize, I'm sure, but would they maybe shoot Rita right in front of me? Was she expandable? Collateral? Had they already shot Kyra?

This was scary. If they were connected to Diego Correra, which, c'mon, how the hell could they not be, there's no way the bounty on my head wasn't astronomical. These bastards were willing to shoot my eight-year-old daughter in bed. In Texas. In the United States. So I seriously doubted there would be any sort of moral hesitation about destroying lives out here.

"Take off your clothes," said Captain Sleazy to Rita.

I knew it. He had a few minutes alone. A few minutes before his police chief would arrive. He knew his bounty was already in the bank, and he wanted to get the most out of this rare assignment.

"Your pants, bitch," said the Captain.

"Don't do it," I told her.

"I'm going to count down from five."

He clicked the hammer on his revolver and aimed it at the back of my head. His leverage against Rita.

"Take off your clothes," he said to her again.

"Don't do it," I told Rita again. "He's bluffing."

"Five."

I just wanted to picture my daughters. Just them. Just to tell them I was about to be with Daddy really soon.

"Four."

I pictured the old living room. The one Christmas when the

tree fell over and we all started laughing because the star landed in a bowl of oatmeal. But my daughter—she was now saying something to me. In my head.

"Three."

She was saying, "Not yet."

"Two."

Not yet.

"One..."

And just as, I swear to God, I saw his finger begin to tighten on the trigger, a door swung open.

Kyra.

And she grabbed Sleazy's muzzle.

And, *bam,* the gun of Double Chin went off and fired a bullet at the left shoulder of Lieutenant Rita Ramirez. Within two steps Kyra had broken her opponent's neck with a judo move, had pulled someone down, flipped him forward, and his body along with his head hit the unforgiving pavement at such an incredibly wrong angle, he was done. Forever.

And we were just getting started.

I rolled backward, trying to move in whatever way my enemy least anticipated, and grabbed the leg of Sergeant Double Chin while still on my back. My foot cocked under his left kneecap just before kicking upward along his thigh as hard as I could, dragging the arch of my foot along his leg, taking his kneecap along for the ride.

He gasped in pain.

His day was over.

Kyra had already grabbed the revolver from the captain and aimed it the throat of the third guy as the fourth guy was trying to wrestle it from her. She was fighting two men at once.

I finished Double Chin with as many forearms to the nose as my controlled rage would allow, which soon rendered him inept so that I could turn to help Kyra, who had already finished off both of her assailants, freeing me to help Rita. So we could get the hell out of there.

Rita didn't look good. Her shoulder was pretty much a half-serving of lasagna thanks to the horrendous gouge of the gun-shot. But she was focused. Maintaining her breathing. And was already up on one knee. Ready for me to yell the cue.

"Move out!"

We got up underneath Rita's good arm, her right one, and helped her rise for what just might be our final sprint. I grabbed a pistol from one of the unconscious hombres, and then we were dashing back through the doorway that Kyra emanated from. A small house. Heading out through the owner's front stoop, *muchas gracias,* where we now had at least a one-minute head start on the rest of the gang. There was nobody in front of us. Nobody behind us. A three-person hydra—we were run-ning our six-legged asses off.

Then I looked over at Rita.

She was smiling.

Not ear-to-ear. But a slight smirk. Smiling.

Kyra and I traded the *uh oh* eye contact. Was she delirious? Los-ing consciousness?

No.

Rita had something in her hand. Something precious that I for-got to grab from the alley in my adrenaline haste, something that was going to revolutionize our situation for good.

She had Double Chin's cell phone.

CHAPTER 34

ON THE MOVE, RUNNING, sprinting, losing a little speed (because, let's face it, we're not goddamn Terminators, although Kyra's a suspected candidate), we were now covered in Rita's blood, some of my blood, and a whole lot of blood from the four inert hombres back in the alley.

It was time to make the call.

I took Double Chin's cell phone and dialed the only special number I had that might function outside the United States. "Bakery Blue Three," I said after the line connected, then paused and slowly stated the following, "The wedding should be held in Mexico City."

We were still running. I was doing my best to enunciate.

"Repeat...the wedding should be held in Mexico City."

This was the evacuation code. It would supposedly—if it worked, which would be a certified miracle since the goddamn number was issued to me two years ago—identify who I am, how many people needed rescuing, and where that rescuing needed to happen. It would thereby elicit an immediate one-time no-questions-asked response consisting of either a ten-thousand-dollar cash deposit to the nearest Western Union, or a ride in a Learjet.

I was waiting on the reply. *The wedding planner has to check on the budget.* That means money is coming. *The wedding planner has to check on the weather.* That means the jet. It's an SOS call that I was never supposed to make. It represented the last favor I could ever ask of anyone at the Pentagon. I'd earned it, trust me, years ago, but the person who felt I'd earned it was probably not at the same desk anymore. Probably didn't answer the same line. In fact, I didn't even hear either one of those code phrases stated back to me.

Instead I got a long pause and then the following:

"Rooftop. Hilton. Nineteen minutes."

It was a man's voice. Meek, almost. Definitely not jolly. Definitely not open to a chat. And then the call ended.

Of course, I tried to dial it back. You're not supposed to, but I tried. And of course my efforts got me the infamous *number is no longer in service* message. In Spanish.

"The Hilton?" questioned Kyra.

There could be two million Hiltons in Mexico City. Or three. Or *ocho*. Or...I don't know. This town is, after all, the second largest damn city in the Western Hemisphere. Why would there be just one stupid Hilton?

"Nineteen minutes," said Kyra, glancing at the clock on the phone. "Eighteen," she corrected herself, as we apparently just spent a full minute worrying about how many minutes we had.

"Gotta be the downtown," said Rita. Her last gasp of verbiage before slipping into delirium again. She was losing blood.

"We need a cab," I said.

No cab would stop for us. Fortunately, we did have enough mileage laid behind us to be within running distance of the downtown hotel location, which meant, yup, more running.

With two minutes to spare, we limped into the hotel's lobby. We were promptly greeted, or should I say, intercepted, by the concierge, who took one look at our triple serving of bad news and already wished we were pre-deleted from his average Tuesday.

"I need roof access," I told him.

"Uh...roof...?" questioned the concierge, before telling me, "I'm sorry, señora, but there is a private party on the terrace right now and the only way to access the roof is to walk through the—"

My gun pressed into his dick. Secretly. So no one else could see. Just me and him, near each other. With my gun. Quietly aimed. And everyone still smiling that fake vacation staff smile.

"*Aquí está mi pistola,*" I said all calm and ex-wifey. "So let me tell you again. Tell you. Not ask. *Tell*...you...I need roof access."

He was already sweating. Poor kid. I bet he's from a nicer part of town where guns and shit aren't the local currency. He seemed gentle, like an avid computer user or someone who played piano in college. "Uh," was his response.

"And make sure we aren't stopped...because if we're stopped...the first thing I'm gonna do is remove your *pito.*"

"*Claro,*" he said.

"Ninety seconds," I informed him. "I want to be up there in ninety seconds."

And he immediately led the three of us past his security group.

I had let him glance down and see my gun. That it was there. I let him see that it was pointing toward his *pito*. I did not let him see that it was out of bullets. That wasn't important now. We were marched through the lobby into an elevator. The four of us. He wisely tried to shoo away a couple of security guys who wanted to sniff around our odd aura. The thing about nice hotels in financially challenged regions of the world is they have a ghastly armada of obsequious service staff, grinning and attentive, gawking at each step you take. Rita's blood was everywhere. On her. On me. On Kyra. We looked like a car accident.

"Is there something wrong?" said one of the security guards.

Our clever concierge spoke without hesitation. "They're doing a Shakespeare...uh...show...for the party upstairs. *No hay problema.*"

The elevator doors closed. We were alone. Thirty seconds.

We might have fooled the lobby staff with the *Macbeth* thing, but, walking through an elegant dining room on the twenty-sixth floor, with classical music piped in and a five-course meal clanking around while snooty tourists looked over at us was not going over well.

I didn't care.

We crossed to a third set of stairs and started walking up to the roof.

"I want your landing pad lights on," I said to our concierge.

"My what?" he replied.

"For the helicopter."

"Ten seconds," said Kyra.

"We don't have a landing pad," he said to me.

"What?"

The door opened. And, yup, there was the roof. The roof, with mostly gravel and some giant air-conditioner units and giant fans.

And that's it.

No landing pad. No landing *area.*

"Rope," said Kyra, announcing that this was gonna be one bitch of an extract.

Rita was passed out at this point. Were they going to lower a harness to us, whoever they were?

Right at the nineteen-minute mark, a *Noticias 6* helicopter emerged from behind another skyscraper, growling with its noisy blades, pulling up to a hover above our roof, to present us with a glorious sight for sore eyes. Our escape vehicle.

The pilot probably had no idea who the hell we were but I'm

guessing what he did know was that his boss owed some kind of mafia-type favor to my boss, whoever *that* might be at this point. Didn't matter. Orders were orders. He looked at us, knowing he was obligated.

The rope ladder descended. Yes, a rope ladder, like, to climb a tree fort. And Rita roused from her drowsy delirium to gather her strength for one last surge of effort. She's such a trooper. Kyra climbed alongside her, two rungs behind, cupping her upward with her body as they both ascended, grip by grip, the fifteen rungs to heaven.

I was about to go next but I stopped to shake my concierge's hand: "I appreciate this more than you know...I uh..." Tired and worn out, I couldn't think of jack shit to say to him so I stated the only sagacious thing I could think of. "Stay in school. And don't do drugs."

Once inside the 'copter, the pilot flew us directly east. I had been on the verge of unconsciousness for many hours now, barely having a sense that, yes, east was toward the main airport, that, yes, this was the extraction we were counting on, that, no, I would not get a chance to pass out because, no, things were not about to get any simpler for the world of Amanda.

Not at all.

CHAPTER 35

I WOKE UP WITH a three-year-old girl staring at me. Rita's daughter. In Rita's living room. I was on Rita's couch. Her little imp was pointing to my phone. "It keeps winging," she said as she got my attention and walked off, her mission accomplished.

I squinted, looking for whatever she was talking about, thinking at least someone was accomplishing missions in my peer group. I saw my phone. Thirty-seven missed calls, thirty-three of which were from the same number. The Fat Man.

I dialed him right away. He answered right away. Uh oh.

"Colonel Collins, welcome back."

"Listen," I said, groggy, but ready to verbally obliterate him.

"No, wait," he interrupted. "Sorry, no, there's no time. Diego is making moves. We have a known location on him. A banquet."

Silence.

I sat there trying to figure out what to say. I'd been gone for, what, one single nap? This was after sprinting through the streets of the most violent city in North America, sprinting, not jogging, *sprinting,* after being borderline tortured by my former employer, after torching three drug crop fields, after the ransacking of my garage, and after the DEA threat to lock me up.

I barely had a sense of who was who anymore, as in who's actually on my team.

"We wanna make a move," said the Fat Man. "Now. This evening."

I still didn't say anything.

"I really shouldn't get into it but..." He hesitated, then he mumbled to himself, "Fuck my fucked-up life." He was already regretting what he was about to say next. "I'm sure you got random presumptions going through your head right now, wondering who the hell I am, whether my intel is legit, why the hell I haven't pinpointed Diego before, why the hell I stay hidden while you're out there in the field get—"

"I'm in."

Silence.

"What?" he replied. He wasn't ready for those two words.

"You had me at 'fuck my fucked-up life,' " I told him. "I'm in."

Minutes later I was standing across the kitchen counter from Kyra. It was a short phone call with the Fat Man so it only took me several seconds to tell her all I knew.

Her response wasn't nearly as enthusiastic as mine. "Are you serious? Total no."

"This could be our only chance," I replied.

"The the Fat Man? Yeah. I ain't buyin' what he's sellin'."

"He said Diego is reactionary. You know what that means? You know what Diego's being reactionary to? Us. Our little waltz through Iztapalapa. We rattled him. *We* did."

"Is that what the Fat Man told you? The same Fat Man who probably sent us there in the first place? Almost got Rita's arm blown off? She's fine, by the way."

I stood there, formulating in my mind the most reasonable explanation I could think of for what was a very unreasonable hunch about him.

But Kyra didn't let me continue.

"Y'know what, it doesn't matter," she said, tone shifted. "If you trust him, I trust him." She saw something in me. Or maybe she just saw me being me, standing there. "I don't need to know what's going on in there." She pointed to my head. "Just tell me where to aim and feed me an MRE."

She turned to head back to her bedroom. She needed what sleep she could get.

CHAPTER 36

ALREADY LATE FOR THE mission prep, I did something I never let myself do before a combat outing. I drove my truck out to Serenity Meadows. Yes, that's a cemetery here in town. You can always tell when something's the name of a cemetery. It sounds like someone tried to put a couple of nice words together in reference to the saddest place on earth.

I don't usually do this before missions. Visit my family. I don't usually kick my heart around like that. But I had something to say I hadn't said before. A question, really.

Their gravesites were near a nice elm tree at the far end of the knoll. I had a box of chocolates for my older daughter. A box of crayons for my younger. And a bottle of A.1. Original Sauce for my husband. Our running joke. Or my running joke. He loved the stuff. Practically drank it. Which repulsed me when he was alive. But now I miss it. I miss the label. I miss the smell. I miss him.

"I...uh...I didn't come here for a good-bye," I said, standing across from his headstone. "I...uh...I just want to just make sure nothing is left unsaid."

I'm not much for communicating beyond the grave and so forth, but I tell ya, there's something real about it. Whenever I need a response from him, I swear, the wind will rustle every tree on the hillside. He speaks to me through the country. That's who he was. Is. A quiet, natural man. And I just needed to find out one last thing from him.

Did you know I was doing this for you?

"You were my favorite person of all time," I said to him. "And...Sorry I brought this tornado upon our family. But I just need to know...if *you* know...that I did it because I wanted to be...to be the person you always admired."

I wanted to be a good Amanda.

My husband's wife.

I needed him to know that. Because there was a strong chance I would never have this conversation again. I could get killed on this one. Not just based on the high danger level, but because I was starting to get careless during battle. I was starting to be less self-preserving. I glimpsed it in Mexico City: a willingness to die. Which is fine, I guess; but the deeper issue was starting to loom on my peripherals: *I don't know if they send souls of people like me upward or downward.* What's in the cards for a former mother who runs around the Western Hemisphere killing people? Shooting enough people to elicit retaliation against her own family? I don't think my soul goes to heaven for that.

So I seriously doubt I'll get reunited with my family up there. But that's fine. I just need my husband to know that when I don't show up, it wasn't for lack of trying. Which sounds like a pity party, table for one, but it's not. I just need them never to wonder how much I loved them.

I put the steak sauce on the base of the stone. I looked up toward the clouds in the distance, felt the breeze rise across one of those spectacular cloud-filled sunsets that looks like the portal to divinity.

"Dear Lord," I said out loud in prayer, "I don't have the proper words to say all this but I pray that you forgive me what I'm about to do." And then I added, "I'm about to finish my life story." And then, "One way or another."

I leaned down and placed a kiss on top of each gravestone. The wind did come up. But it didn't drown out my final whisper.

"Good-bye, my darlings."

CHAPTER 37

BACK IN THE SUPPLY tunnel behind our garage, I was prepping my new HK416. Rendezvous was at 6:45 p.m. And the birds were on time. Whatever dread I had that Fat Man might screw me over was entirely dispelled when I emerged onto the field. Two Bell Huey helicopters were there. That was expected. But what was truly a shock, what brought tears to my eyes, and I'm not a crier, is what was *in* those helicopters. My crew.

My crew.

Nearly half my original platoon was suited up. Locked and loaded.

"What Diego did to you is beyond criminal," said the radio operator. Marcus. My first friend from basic training. "We can't let it go unchecked."

The others nodded in agreement.

I had a lump in my throat. I was already beyond emotional. Then, when I got in, I saw Rita there, shoulder bandaged, hobbling, barely able to get her fatigues to fit. She looked like a medical training video. I couldn't hide the disapproval on my face.

But she wasn't interested in my face. "Can't keep me out of this fight, Colonel."

"No, no, no," I said, ready to begin orating my commonsense dissertation on the importance of health and safety. "You need to stay here so that—"

She cut me off, "You can't keep me out." And with that, she yanked the door hatch shut, closing us all in the cabin to make her point. And then stared at me with enough impenetrable stubbornness to change my mind on the spot.

"No, ma'am," I agreed. "I can't."

CHAPTER 38

WE WERE ROARING ALONG at 110 miles per hour back into Mexico. I might as well buy a condo there. Feels like my second home. No, wait, first home. I spent more time there than I did in Texas. In my head, anyway.

After an hour of chitchat among the crew, we began to quiet down. Mission protocol was to start focusing mentally on what was ahead for each of us. Focusing on the execution of the basics.

"All right, platoon, listen up," I said over the radio. "The intel on the compound is that it's occupied by both hostile and neutral persons. But I'm not interested in being morally correct on this one. I'm not interested in you fine folks losing life or limb. The ROE on this op is fire away."

"Drop zone in sight," said the pilot. "Range to target six clicks."

My crew started murmuring to each other in reaction but I kept talking. "Expect every single thing in that place to want you dead on arrival. Even the chef'll throw his fork at you if he can. Shoot to kill."

And that's exactly what we did. Ten minutes later, we hadn't even commenced our fast-rope insertion, and we were already embroiled in an air-to-ground gunfight. We were firing on their watchtower. They were firing on our broadside.

We were at war with Diego.

Fast roping works best when you can destroy whatever is shooting at you before you drop down next to it and cuddle. In our case it was a genuine watchtower. Two enemies with M24 rifles. Mid-conversation, mid-smoke, they looked up, saw us on the horizon, and shot us up. We saw them and returned service.

The ROE, the rules of engagement, were wide open for us. My teams had been so battered by Diego over the years, they were now playing the feud game. Scars were deep. Memories were long.

Show up and shoot.

I slid down the rope and greeted the ground along with a flood of bullets from the patio. Some douche decided to buy himself a Gatling gun and mount it by his pool. That's what was now besieging me and Marcus as we were the first on the ground.

However, with two quick shots from her rifle, Kyra had pierced the guy's skull open from high up in the doorway of our helicopter. That's my girl. Allowing me to crouch down, take point, and fire as many rounds into the gazebo as possible.

They weren't precise shots. I was aiming for where I expected soldiers to be. The entire picnic crowd was scrambling. We definitely had caught them with their pants down. There wasn't one single guard who looked ready for a fight. Their own intel, if they even had any, was that skies were clear, weather was balmy, and the roasted pork was lightly salted.

The bad news for us, though, was that the whole place was crawling with families.

Kids.

Ugh. My team was cleared to shoot at will but none of us was willing to blast at a crowd of kids. Even with all the enemy guards ducking down and running back into the shadows among the scattering families, we still didn't have the stomach to shoot into a civilian throng. Which, *ahem,* was a recipe for a difficult afternoon.

"Pressing forward," I yelled. "Condor Five, gimme cover on the patio."

The gunner in the Huey fired his Vulcan 20mm, which is a big weapon that makes a big noise and desecrates everything it sees, spitting out the kind of big bullet hailstorm that devours concrete. He lit up the pool deck as a show of force, as a poker move, to intimidate enemy shooters who were hiding in the family crowd and motivate them to take deeper cover rather than hold a line. Those enemies weren't, after all, 100 percent sure we *wouldn't* fire into them. (We wouldn't, but they didn't know that.) Which meant we now had about ten solid seconds of hesitation on their part when we could rush inside the hacienda.

"PRESS!" I yelled.

And I darted along a pinball path of whatever items of cover I could find. A lawn chair, a lawn table, the buffet itself, a cart, some garbage cans, a moped. Aiming my gun to take any precise shot possible toward the cluster of enemies, but not finding a single clean target, given that each thug was eclipsed by a screaming nine-year-old or a terrified nanny.

Where the hell is Diego?

As my platoon scurried into better positions, covering one another, taking out stray guards who couldn't retreat fast enough, I began to scan the area for the Holy Grail himself. Our radio code name for him was quite fitting, by the way.

"I have no visual on Dickbag," I said into my radio. "Condor Two, make sure he doesn't have wheels."

"Copy that," replied the pilot.

My primary Huey ascended up out of its hover and flew about a hundred yards down the hill toward the mansion's parking lot, where a bunch of Escalades and Mercedes were parked.

Wham! Not anymore!

One by one, each vehicle was blown to Neptune by our guy in the sky. Hellfire missiles will do that to your morning commute. Which, however, still didn't bring me my Dickbag.

Where was he?

I now stood in the hacienda's living room, searching among the cowering faces for any sign of my nemesis. Please God, tell me this S.O.B. is actually here. I kept thinking to myself I can't do this again. I can't drag my comrades into hell, burn them in combat, drench them in foreign and domestic blood, then send them back home, baked and bruised, only to sit by a fireplace years from now and say wistfully, *Yeah, whelp, we did our best, tough racket.*

Erase that thought, Amanda.

A cartel bandito in a cowboy hat spun from behind a wall with a 12-gauge aimed right for my chest, just as I squeezed the trigger on my HK first, downing him.

Close call.

I pressed forward even more, entering the middle rooms of the massive ranch. I think this place was actually one of Diego's seven mansions. Seven.

More bullets flew past my head, screaming their airy little trajectories, as I barely ducked in time. I couldn't believe how distracted I was getting. This particular shooter was on the far side of the room—a dude with a superb nickel-plated .45. Must be nice to be rich. I spun up and hammered three quick shots at him, catching his face all three times. Which scared his buddy, who was already having second thoughts about loitering in public during a Marine invasion.

I entered the main dining room.

And finally found myself dwelling in a moment I'd salivated over and dreamed about, craved and feared and loathed and talked about, for nearly a decade.

Him.

I had come around a large wooden pillar, moving low, moving while crouched, in case anyone was anticipating where my *cabeza* would appear.

"Ten cuidado," said Diego Correra.

He looked different from what I imagined. I almost didn't perceive him as him. And you know why? This is going to sound weird. Because he looked exactly like his pictures. I never expected it to be so real. So vivid. Like seeing a celebrity. An evil superstar.

It was a bit surreal and robbed me of my focus for a moment.

"Slow!" he said.

He had a hostage. He had a girl by the throat. I had discovered him before he even had a chance to reload a gun. We were in a standoff. He had a jungle knife and was holding it against the jugular of a tall, skinny adolescent.

"Drop the blade!" I yelled at him.

He didn't. He repositioned himself so she became his full armor. He knew his angles. My guess is he's done this before. She literally blocked every square inch of his body I could've had a shot at.

I kept my aim at a small sliver of nothingness lurking just outside the edge of his neck, on the off chance the girl squirms even a tiny bit sideways and exposes a lethal target for me.

She didn't. But she could. She might.

And there we stood.

I doubt I meant as much to him as he did to me, but I could tell this wasn't an ordinary encounter for Dickbag Correra. He was sizing me up. Finally getting a chance to put the face to the name.

"Be careful how you aim, Amanda, you might hit *me*."

I had to think of a way to lull him a bit. Defuse the tension on his end. "Let's just relax, Diego, I don't want you dead," I lied.

"Drop the gun, or I cut her open right in front of you."

Dear God, please tell me that's not his own daughter.

"I'll poke the bottom of her brain," he said. "Right in front of you. And her coma will be on your conscience. Forever."

"My orders are to bring you in alive, Diego. You're no good dead. Let's just walk out of here. Both of us. No harm."

He didn't respond.

"What do you say," I said to him. "Deal?"

There was a ton of gunfire occurring behind me. My estimation is that most of the families were taking deep cover at this point, which meant my platoon would be trying to overtake the fight. I could hear our HK submachine guns and I could hear enemy AK-47s. Everyone shooting at everyone.

Diego was growing skittish in front of me. He could tell his hombres outside were losing. I could see it on his face. Which meant he was becoming a man of desperation. Which was not ideal. For either of us.

"Drop the knife!" I yelled at him.

"Wait."

"Drop the knife!"

"Listen!"

And just when I thought I might watch a grown man crumple, he did the unthinkable. He plunged the blade into her throat. Up her chin, into her head, twisted the blade so the hole became a cross. He did it because he knew I would stutter for just that one split-second as my chess opponent committed a move I just didn't think professionally possible, and then he, Diego, descended down an entrance to a wine cellar, disappearing from the room, just as I let three bursts from my gun smash uselessly against the wall above him.

Dear Lord.

The girl slumped forward.

Rita came running in. "Medic!" she called out, hurrying over to tend to the girl. As Kyra ran right for the wine cellar entrance, driven by killer instincts, knowing exactly what had just happened without even seeing it, firing into the dark entrance, then turning back to check on me.

She called into the radio headset. "Condor Five, I have positive ID on Dickbag, heading into a wine cellar on the southwest corner."

Kyra saw me frozen there. She knew I was having a moment.

"Colonel, form up?" she asked me.

She was waiting for me to organize a posse, to form up. You don't want to just ram yourself down into a dark tunnel alone with a psychopath. Going in solo would certainly mean getting shot or walking into explosives.

"Colonel, can we form up?" Kyra asked again, flipping her night vision goggles on. Diego was running as fast as he could down along a tunnel that was guaranteed to lead him wherever we didn't want him to be.

But I didn't wait for that posse. I didn't even call it in. I ran straight down into the darkness. Straight after him.

Now or never.

CHAPTER 39

THERE WERE LOTS OF kids down here. And moms. And maids. And chefs. It was unlit. It was one of those tunnels we hated to raid. Chaotic. Confusing. Dark. Wrong.

I was in kill mode. Bearing a heightened sense of detail. Whenever one of the bandits ahead of me, hidden among the sporadic pockets of cowering civilians, would rise up and point a gun at me, I would end him. One shot. Forehead. Bam. Dead.

Heightened sense.

I kept moving. Kept pursuing. I'd entered Hades itself. Small torches here and there. The pervasive sounds of various women crying in fear set against a backdrop of eerie silence. I could hear my own breathing. Like jogging laps on the track back at Pendleton. Just hearing myself inhale. Just finding the calm in the respiratory rhythm. Exhale. I descended a few stairs to enter a deeper corridor, this one intermittently lit by bare bulbs, creating darkness punctuated by semidarkness punctuated by darkness again. I could see a few women up ahead fleeing from my oncoming presence but no sign of Diego.

Then, bam, another shot from my gun, piercing another one of the thugs who was crouched among the kids.

Heightened.

"Colonel! Slow down!" called Kyra from way behind.

I had vastly outpaced her, violating mission protocol, letting my emotions get to me, opting for a dangerous tactic, but I was in a different consciousness right now. My value system had been inverted. I didn't care about my own safety. I just needed Diego down. More than I needed my own life, I needed his. I needed to possess it.

I emerged into a room, a sort of cave or antechamber, with three women huddled on the floor off to the side in an anonymous clump. They had their faces buried, their long dresses covering their bodies and their limbs.

He had to come through here. He had to. But I couldn't see him in the next stretch of passage. And it was a long stretch.

There's no way he sprinted that fast. That would be two hundred meters in under ten seconds. That's faster than the Olympics. And while I was standing there, overanalyzing, overcalculating, over-thinking, as Amanda always does, it happened.

I heard a pop.

The front of my chest poofed with red air. Red spray. Like I'd been hit from behind by a sledgehammer.

I had been shot. From the rear.

By one of those women.

By someone who was *dressed* as a woman.

By Diego. In a dress.

I could hear him reload. Shotgun blast. The only reason I was still standing was because he fired too close behind me, missing my heart but hitting my shoulder instead. Shotgun shells hurt. I could now answer that question whenever someone asked me at parties. *Hey, does that shit hurt?* Yes, it goddamn does. While he reloaded, while this eternal split-second continued to elapse, I spun around and one-handedly rifle-butted him in the jaw with my HK. His head snapped back, then he lurched forward and bear-hugged me in a full tackle. The women shrieked. They must have been his wives or sisters. Or both. We started to wrestle. Clawing at each other. It wasn't the cinematic fistfight you'd pay twenty bucks to watch at the IMAX. No. It was two people scraping their talons at each other's everything, trying to get any kind of physiological advantage. Him dead-tired from sprinting, me dead-tired from being alive the past decade.

And that's when the first ray of dawn smiled upon my cloudy life.

I cracked his wrist bone backward making him yelp in pain, then bent his elbow backward, hyperextending it. Then broke it. Broke his arm.

And broke him.

He was done.

Rendered inept. Fight over. He was thoroughly at my mercy, as I stood there maintaining my superior leverage on his fractured elbow, leaving him now gasping on his knees.

He was waiting for me to fire my pistol at him. I had a sidearm. Available. But I hadn't even taken it out of my holster.

I had him.

When he saw this, saw what was not happening, he did something I didn't expect. He started laughing. And after a half minute of this, this genuine amusement, this borderline inexplicable joy, I had to know.

"What's so funny?" I asked.

"Hahaha..." he petered out, to collect himself, to say the following. "I kill your friends, I kill your husband, I kill your ugly daughter, her ugly sister... I do all that... and you don't have the balls to do anything back."

"I'm above you," I said to him. "I'm above your world. I'm putting you in jail."

"*I own the damn jail, you lonely cunt!*" He spat blood on the floor. Proudly. "I'm already free. While you stand there! Frozen like a statue. Like a statue commemorating my power. I'm already free. That's how untouchable I am! Because I am to your people the most precious thing your country could ever want. I am *stability*, you gaping cow." He stood up, gathering Socratic steam. "Your bosses...and your bosses' bosses...will never let me die. In fact...I'm gonna tell them that they should take you by the hair and—"

BAM!

He dropped to the floor. Dead.

Shot by Kyra.

Smoking gun in her hand. She didn't move for a moment. She stood there catching her breath. Then she leaned over to whisper to the bloody pulp of his skull: "Amanda Collins is a lawful person...but I'm not."

And there we stood. She and I. With Diego on the floor.

We got him.

Each in our own way.

We got him.

EPILOGUE

THAT WAS ELEVEN months ago. That was also one preg-
nancy ago. Rita, the baby machine, got busy with Mr. Rita several
weeks after that mission, and cranked out another baby girl. Gorgeous enough to earn her the name Kyra Jane. She was born right
in their house because Rita's womb was either too efficient or too
lazy to wait for the hospital ride.

Kyra, the original version, started dating one of the firefighters
from church. Theoretically it was a courtship, but they were going on those ambiguous non-date dates where nobody in the
equation is sure if they're actually on a date or not. And that fog
has lasted six weeks now. Welcome to modern social combat. I
don't miss it.

Me, I was sitting on the porch, clutching two wrenches while
arguing with a carburetor. And that's when a pair of government
feet creaked onto my wooden front steps.

There stood Officer Teeth himself.

Warren Wright.

To be honest, I wasn't even mad. The closure on Diego's case
was handled in such a deft way that my name was kept out of
every single news article and military document. That was my
deepest wish. Anonymity. And I know Wright's department, deep

within the bowels of his behemoth administration, must have made that happen.

"Colonel," he said. His greeting.

"Agent Wright," I said back. Trying to sound cool.

He stood there a moment, probably intending to conjure up small talk to disguise his real purpose, whatever that would be, and looking shy about it. For the first time ever. Shy. "You managed to locate the number five guy on the North American Most Wanted list. And you managed to take him down in the middle of his own army. Never got a chance to say thanks."

"And?"

"And...it was impressive. You must've had help."

Oh, so that's it. "Look, slick, if you're here to try to..."

"No. I'm not here to ask that question."

I heard a familiar rasp in his voice. A twang. Something I couldn't place. He was staring at me. His smirk etched on his face with God's permanent marker. Then I started thinking a thought that just couldn't possibly be true, a thought that occurred to me once a long time ago but got instantly dismissed.

"Then what are you here for?" I asked.

"Well, it's certainly not to get you to betray your source. That would be lame." He sighed. "Fuck my fucked-up life."

I knew it!

"I'm here to buy you a beer," he said.

"You're the Fat Man," I quietly exclaimed, scrutinizing his face, his body, his tailored suit. Refusing to believe it. "No...there's...if you...no..."

And so he came clean. "Third time you and I ever talked on the phone I was trying to think of a decent code name for myself and literally had no idea what to tell you. So...since I had just eaten two pints of Ben & Jerry's...and felt bloated...I figured..." he presented himself, arms outstretched. "Fat Man." He patted his gut for reference, his six-pack. Proud of his irony. "I know it's a bit ironic—"

"No, I can see it."

He stopped. Almost hurt for a second, then saw my deadpan face and infinite sarcasm and started laughing. Then he shifted gears. "Sorry about Mexico City. I had to cooperate with General Claire 'The Hair' Dolan, otherwise she'd sniff me out."

We paused for a moment. We worked well together. It's a shame I had to say no to what I already knew he wanted.

"I'm here to offer you a job," he said.

"I'm retired," I replied.

As usual, Warren Wright wasn't really listening to me. He continued talking as if I hadn't just said whatever I just said. "We have a situation," he informed me. "In Europe. We can't take care of it with proper channels." He cleared his throat. "You're the improper one. You're the one we need."

"You know I'm gonna tell you I'm out. You know I'm gonna tell you my whole career has been a hunt for one man and now that this one man is done, I'm done."

He smirked. Wider.

"Which you're not even hearing," I said, realizing it. I put the carburetor down. I stood up. "Fine. One beer."

"So you're in?"

"No. But I'll let you have the privilege of arguing with me."

"Good," he said, opening the passenger door to his truck for me. He met my eyes and smiled. "I've earned it."

THE SUSPECT IS YOUR
PATIENT, DR. CROSS. . .

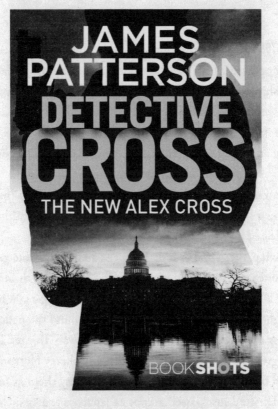

**Read on for an extract of the new story
in the Alex Cross series.**

BREE STONE WAS thirty minutes into her morning exercise and breathing hard as she ran east along a path by the Tidal Basin in Washington, DC. It was a gorgeous spring day in late March, warm with a fragrant breeze.

The Japanese cherry trees that lined the path were in full bloom, attracting early tourists. Bree had to dodge a few of them, but it was so pretty a setting and day that she didn't mind.

She was in her late thirties, but her legs felt stronger than they had when she was just out of college. So did her breathing, and that pleased her. The daily exercise was working.

Leaving the Tidal Basin, Bree cut past the statue of John Paul Jones and jogged in place, waiting to cross 17th Street SE beside a DC bus discharging and loading passengers. When the bus sighed and rolled away, Bree looped around the pedestrians to cross the street, toward the National Sylvan Theater and another grove of blooming cherry trees. The cherry blossoms only peaked once a year and she intended to enjoy them as much as possible. She'd just passed a knot of Japanese tourists when her cell phone rang.

She plucked the phone from the small fanny pack she wore, but did not stop or slow. Bree glanced at the unfamiliar phone number and let her voice mail take the call. She ran on and soon could see a team of National Park Police raising the fifty American flags surrounding the base of the Washington Monument. Her phone rang again, same number.

Irritated, she stopped and answered, "Bree Stone."

"Chief Bree Stone?"

The voice was male. Or was it? The tone wasn't deep.

"Who's calling, please?"

"Your worst nightmare, Chief. There's an IED on the National Mall. You should have answered my first call. Now you only have fifty-eight minutes to figure out where I left it."

The line died. Bree stared at the phone half a beat, then checked her watch. 7:28 a.m. Detonation: 8:26 a.m.? She hit a number on speed dial and surveyed the area, swallowing the impulse to get well off the Mall as fast as possible.

DC Metro Police Chief Jim Michaels answered on the second ring.

"Why is my chief of detectives calling me? I told her to take a few days off."

"I just got an anonymous call, Jim," Bree said. "An IED planted on the National Mall, set to go off at 8:26 a.m. We need to clear the area as fast as possible and bring in the dogs."

In the short silence that followed, Bree thought of something and started sprinting toward the men raising flags.

"Are you sure it wasn't a crank?" Chief Michaels said.

"Do you want to take the chance it isn't a crank?"

Michaels let out a sharp puff of breath and said, "I'll notify National Park and Capitol Hill Police. You sound like you're running. Where are you?"

"On the Mall. Going to high ground to spot the bomber on his way out of Dodge."

IT WAS 7:36 A.M. when the elevator doors opened.

Bree rushed out onto the observation platform of the Washington Monument, some five hundred and fifty-four feet above the National Mall. She carried a chattering US Park Service Police radio, tuned to a frequency being used by all FBI, US Capitol Police, and DC Metro Police personnel rapidly responding to the situation.

She had a pair of binoculars lent to her by the officers guarding the closed monument. Balking at her initial demand to be let in, they had given her a hard time while checking her story.

Then the sirens had started wailing from all angles, and their commander came back with direct orders to open the monument and let her ride to the top. Bree had lost eight minutes in the process, but pushed that frustration to the back of her mind. They had fifty minutes to find the bomb.

Bree went straight to the high slit windows cut in the west wall of the monument, and peered through the binoculars toward the Lincoln Memorial and the long, rectangular pool that reflected its image and that of the Washington Monument. When she'd started to run toward the towering limestone obelisk, she'd hoped to get high enough to catch sight of someone fleeing the Mall or acting strangely.

But too much time had passed. The bomber would have beat feet, gotten as far away as possible, wouldn't he? That was the logical thought, but Bree wondered if he might be the kind of sicko to stick around, admire his explosive handiwork.

Even at this early hour there were scores of people running, walking, and riding on the paths that crisscrossed the Mall and paralleled the reflecting pool. Others were standing as if transfixed by the chorus of sirens coming closer and closer.

Bree pivoted, strode across the observation deck to the east wall where she could look out toward the US Capitol, and triggered the radio mic.

"This is Metro CoD Stone," she said, scanning the open park between the Smithsonian museums. "I can see hundreds of people still on the Mall, and who knows how many more that I can't see because of the trees. Move officers to 17th, 15th, Madison Drive Northwest, Jefferson Drive Southwest, Ohio Drive Southwest, and 7th Northwest, 4th Northwest, and 3rd Northwest. Work civilian evacuation from the middle of the Mall to the north and south. Keep it quick and orderly. We don't want to cause panic."

"Roger that, Chief," the dispatcher came back.

Bree waited until she heard the dispatcher call out her orders, then said, "Block all traffic through the Mall north and south and Constitution and Independence Avenues from 3rd to Ohio."

"That's already been ordered, Chief," the dispatcher said.

"Status of K-9 and bomb squads?"

"FBI, Metro, and Park Police K-9s en route, but traffic's snarling. Metro's ETA on 15th is two minutes. Bomb squads say five minutes out, but could be longer."

Longer? She cursed inwardly. Looked down at the flags fluttering and noted their direction and stiffness.

She triggered the mic again. "Tell all K-9 patrols that the wind here is south-southwest, maybe ten miles an hour. They'll want to work from northeast angles."

"Roger that," the dispatcher said.

Bree checked her watch. 7:41. They had forty-five minutes to find and defuse the IED.

Gazing out, her mind racing, Bree realized she knew something about the bomber. He or she had used the term IED, Improvised Explosive Device, not bomb. IED was a US military term. Was the bomber ex-military? Current military?

Then again, Bree had seen and heard the term often enough on news and media reports. But why would a civilian use that term instead of bomb? Why be so specific?

Her phone rang. Chief Michaels.

"Because of your unique location and perspective, we're giving you overall command of the situation, Chief," he said by way of greeting. "K-9, bomb, and tactical squads will operate at your call after advising you of the options."

Bree didn't miss a beat. "FBI and Capitol Hill?"

"Waiting on your orders."

"Thank you for the confidence, sir."

"Prove it," he said, and hung up.

For the next six minutes, as she monitored radio chatter, Bree roamed back and forth, looking east and west, seeing cruiser after cruiser turn sideways to block access to Constitution and Independence Avenues where they ran parallel to the Mall.

At 7:49, twenty-one minutes after the bomber's phone call, mounted police appeared and cantered their horses the length of the Mall, shouting to everyone to leave the quickest way possible. Other patrol cars cruised Independence, Constitution, and Madison, using their bullhorns to spur the evacuation.

Despite Bree's hope for calm, the police horses and bullhorns were clearly seeding panic. Joggers turned and sprinted north and south off the Mall. Fathers grabbed their kids and ran. Moms pushed baby carriages helter-skelter. Tourists poured like ants out of the Lincoln Memorial and left the Vietnam and World War II Memorials in droves.

Bree kept the binoculars pressed tight to her eyes, looking for someone lingering, someone wanting a last look at the spot where the bomb was stashed, or positioned to remotely detonate the device.

But she saw no one that set off alarm bells.

The son of a bitch is gone, she thought. *Long gone.*

ALSO BY JAMES PATTERSON

ALEX CROSS NOVELS
Along Came a Spider
Kiss the Girls
Jack and Jill
Cat and Mouse
Pop Goes the Weasel
Roses are Red
Violets are Blue
Four Blind Mice
The Big Bad Wolf
London Bridges
Mary, Mary
Cross
Double Cross
Cross Country
Alex Cross's Trial (*with Richard DiLallo*)
I, Alex Cross
Cross Fire
Kill Alex Cross
Merry Christmas, Alex Cross
Alex Cross, Run
Cross My Heart
Hope to Die
Cross Justice
Cross the Line

THE WOMEN'S MURDER CLUB SERIES
1st to Die
2nd Chance (*with Andrew Gross*)
3rd Degree (*with Andrew Gross*)
4th of July (*with Maxine Paetro*)
The 5th Horseman (*with Maxine Paetro*)

The 6th Target (*with Maxine Paetro*)
7th Heaven (*with Maxine Paetro*)
8th Confession (*with Maxine Paetro*)
9th Judgement (*with Maxine Paetro*)
10th Anniversary (*with Maxine Paetro*)
11th Hour (*with Maxine Paetro*)
12th of Never (*with Maxine Paetro*)
Unlucky 13 (*with Maxine Paetro*)
14th Deadly Sin (*with Maxine Paetro*)
15th Affair (*with Maxine Paetro*)
16th Seduction (*with Maxine Paetro*)

DETECTIVE MICHAEL BENNETT SERIES
Step on a Crack (*with Michael Ledwidge*)
Run for Your Life (*with Michael Ledwidge*)
Worst Case (*with Michael Ledwidge*)
Tick Tock (*with Michael Ledwidge*)
I, Michael Bennett (*with Michael Ledwidge*)
Gone (*with Michael Ledwidge*)
Burn (*with Michael Ledwidge*)
Alert (*with Michael Ledwidge*)
Bullseye (*with Michael Ledwidge*)

PRIVATE NOVELS
Private (*with Maxine Paetro*)
Private London (*with Mark Pearson*)
Private Games (*with Mark Sullivan*)
Private: No. 1 Suspect (*with Maxine Paetro*)
Private Berlin (*with Mark Sullivan*)

Private Down Under (*with Michael White*)
Private L.A. (*with Mark Sullivan*)
Private India (*with Ashwin Sanghi*)
Private Vegas (*with Maxine Paetro*)
Private Sydney (*with Kathryn Fox*)
Private Paris (*with Mark Sullivan*)
The Games (*with Mark Sullivan*)
Private Delhi (*with Ashwin Sanghi*)

NYPD RED SERIES
NYPD Red (*with Marshall Karp*)
NYPD Red 2 (*with Marshall Karp*)
NYPD Red 3 (*with Marshall Karp*)
NYPD Red 4 (*with Marshall Karp*)

DETECTIVE HARRIET BLUE SERIES
Never Never (*with Candice Fox*)
Fifty Fifty (*with Candice Fox, to be published July 2017*)

STAND-ALONE THRILLERS
Sail (*with Howard Roughan*)
Swimsuit (*with Maxine Paetro*)
Don't Blink (*with Howard Roughan*)
Postcard Killers (*with Liza Marklund*)
Toys (*with Neil McMahon*)
Now You See Her (*with Michael Ledwidge*)
Kill Me If You Can (*with Marshall Karp*)
Guilty Wives (*with David Ellis*)
Zoo (*with Michael Ledwidge*)
Second Honeymoon (*with Howard Roughan*)
Mistress (*with David Ellis*)

Invisible (*with David Ellis*)
The Thomas Berryman Number
Truth or Die (*with Howard Roughan*)
Murder House (*with David Ellis*)
Woman of God (*with Maxine Paetro*)
Hide and Seek
Humans, Bow Down (*with Emily Raymond*)
The Black Book (*with David Ellis*)
Murder Games (*with Howard Roughan*)

BOOKSHOTS
Black & Blue (*with Candice Fox*)
Cross Kill
Private Royals (*with Rees Jones*)
The Trial (*with Maxine Paetro*)
Chase (*with Michael Ledwidge*)
113 Minutes (*with Max DiLallo*)
The Verdict (*with Robert Gold*)
French Kiss (*with Richard DiLallo*)
Taking the Titanic (*with Scott Slaven*)
Killer Chef (*with Jeffrey J. Keyes*)
The Christmas Mystery (*with Richard DiLallo*)
Kidnapped (*with Robert Gold*)
Come and Get Us (*with Shan Serafin*)
Hidden (*with James O. Born*)
The House Husband (*with Duane Swierczynski*)
Malicious (*with James O. Born*)
French Twist (*with Richard DiLallo*)
The Exile (*with Alison Joseph*)
The End (*with Brendan DuBois*)
The Shut In (*with Duane Swierczynski*)
Private Gold (*with Jassy Mackenzie*)
After the End (*with Brendan DuBois*)